Other books by Kerry Gibb

Finalist IAN Book of the Year Awards 2018

Get signed copies of all Kerry Gibb's books from kerrygibb.com! Just scan the QR code below!

THE
ELEPHANT
SQUAD

Kerry Gibb

Published by Packman Publishing.

First edition published in Great Britain in 2022.

Printed and bound in Great Britain at Clays Ltd,
Elcograf S.p.A.

A CIP catalogue record for this title is available from
the British Library.

ISBN: 978-0-9934937-6-8

This novel is fiction. The names, characters and
incidents portrayed in it are from the author's
imagination. Any other resemblance to actual
persons, events, or localities in entirely
coincidental.

For Liam, Jamie, Danny, and Joe
who championed this story every step of the
way.

CLEO

Cleo could hear them all talking about it. She pretended not to care and stared out of the window at the butterfly that landed gracefully on the bush outside. As it brought its wings together like the pages of a book closing, she remembered how she had read once that butterflies represent a feeling of hope. Squinting her eyes at it intently, she willed it to pass some of its positive energy through the window and onto her.

Quickly bored of the bush it had settled

on, the butterfly stretched open its magnificent wings and flew off on its next adventure. Cleo watched enviously as her mind drifted back to her original thoughts. Everyone seemed to know about it – everyone except for the teachers. Cleo could only imagine what it must have been like. The excitement of sneaking over to the new boy to discreetly buy sweets from his secret tuck shop as the flashing lights guided the way. Music so loud that your body involuntarily started to move to the beat as the kids around you danced and chased each other with balloon swords.

The annual school disco had been the main source of excitement for Cleo's classmates for every one of the six years that she had spent at primary school. She had never experienced it herself though, and given that she was now approaching her final year of Summercroft School, she had accepted that she would only ever witness it vicariously as her imagination elaborated on the conversations that she overheard. And the disco on Friday certainly sounded like one that would go down in school gossip history.

Everyone in the class except for Cleo appeared to have been there. All they had had to worry about last Friday evening was what they were going to wear and whether they could sneak on some of their mum's lipstick without her noticing. Whether they should risk their friends laughing at them if they danced to the out-of-date *Birdy-Song* that the fifty-year-old DJ played. And judging from the conversations all around her, the most important decision of the night had been how much pocket money to bring to spend on the forbidden, secret sweets.

The class had stayed stagnant since they had all started in Reception, with their over-sized jumpers and chubby cheeks. But a few months ago, a new boy called Ben Collins had joined them. They had all sat there silent, staring at him like he was a rare, endangered snow leopard, as the teacher buddied him up with Tommy. Cleo remembered feeling jealous that Tommy had been given a new friend without even trying. She would have liked a new friend. Inside school she was friends with everyone and was always included in games of bulldog and manhunt on the playground. But no-one ever invited her to their house anymore, or to their parties.

They had done initially, but the invites became fewer and fewer as the months went on. No-one wanted to waste an invite on the girl who would always say no. She cringed as she remembered the excuses that she had invented when she was younger – excuses that she had concocted courtesy of her *'Contagious Kids'* book. Conjunctivitis... diarrhoea... a verruca. Luckily, she had rapidly used up all the gruesome fictional explanations, and, as time went on, she had opted for the more socially acceptable excuse that she had a swimming lesson or a football club. In reality, she had never kicked a ball in her life – unless you count the time that she had inadvertently walked onto the football pitch one break time and tripped over the ball. And her sole experience of a swimming lesson was her mum shouting words of encouragement as she held onto the edge of her paddling pool in the garden and attempted a very questionable breaststroke kick whilst her tummy scraped the lining at the bottom.

One day, the invites had just stopped all together. No-one had even bothered asking her what she was wearing to the school disco because they all knew that she wouldn't be going.

Cleo wasn't like the other kids. She didn't have brothers or sisters at home, and she didn't have a dad there either. It was just Cleo and her mum. Sometimes, she imagined her mum rushing over to give her a hug when she arrived home from school. In her favourite daydream she could practically smell the cookies that her mum would be baking as their pet dog waited eagerly by her feet, hoping that she would drop one as she pulled them out of the oven, oozing with chocolate chips.

In reality though, the cookies would always be in a bargain 99p packet from the Co-op, and the nearest thing that Cleo had to a pet dog was the toy Pound Puppy that she had been given last Christmas, which came with an adoption certificate. She seriously regretted her decision to call it Carol. At the time, she'd thought that it was a clever play on *'A Christmas Carol'* – a film that she had watched with her mum on Christmas Eve. Now it wasn't Christmas anymore, and she was stuck with a dog called a rubbish name that made it sound like a middle-aged woman. Cleo wanted to change it to something significant like Sapphire, to represent its piercing blue eyes, or Talula because, well just because it sounded both cute and cool at the same time. But no, the closest thing that she had to a pet would always be called Carol as she had written it on the pretend adoption certificate.

For the rest of the afternoon, Cleo struggled to focus as she kept looking at the clock. As soon as the teacher announced that it was home time, she grabbed her bag and coat and, as usual, was first out of the door. She knew that if she made it through the crowds of parents waiting for their kids and kept a fast pace down to the main road, she could make it to the crossing by 3.25pm. Then, as long as the lights turned red within one minute, and the cars stopped to allow her to cross, she could run down the alleyway that led to the ground floor maisonette sat cosily in the middle of its terrace. If all went to plan, she could slot her key into the front door no later than 3.29pm.

'Hello, love, is that you?' her mum called out as she heard the front door slam shut.

'Yes, it's me, Mum. Where are you?'

'I'm in the bathroom, love. Nothing to worry about, but could you come and give me a hand please?'

Running anxiously to the bathroom at the back of the house, Cleo saw her mum sitting on the floor leaning against the bath. She put a big smile on her face as she saw her daughter, but her puffy eyes gave away the truth that she'd been crying.

'Silly, me,' she said, trying to make light of it. 'I slipped when I was getting my toothbrush and can't quite get myself up with these spindly arms.'

Grabbing the wheelchair that sat nonchalantly in the corner of the bathroom, Cleo positioned it next to her mum, securing the brake. Using all her strength, she tucked her arms under her mum's and lifted, just like the physio had taught her.

'Thanks, love. I'm so sorry you had to find me like this.'

'I'm going to stay home from school with you tomorrow, Mum,' Cleo said, feeling guilty that she hadn't been there when her mum had needed her.

'Nonsense, love, you don't need to do that. I'll be fine.'

Cleo didn't argue, but made a promise to herself that she would leave a message on the school answer phone early in the morning before the office staff arrived. She had perfected her adult tone for declaring a sick day years ago. All she had to do was squash her neck into a double chin, which miraculously lowered her voice, and use phrases such as 'regrettably won't be in today' and 'endeavour to return soon'. Adults were so easy to fool when you needed to.

'I'll put some jacket potatoes in the oven for dinner, Mum. Beans and cheese alright with you?'

'Perfect,' replied her mum as she wheeled herself out of the bathroom after her daughter. 'I'll come and chat to you whilst you do it.'

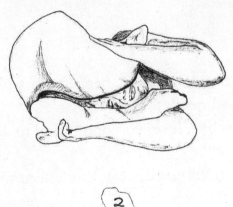

JAYDEN

Banging his pen down on the desk, Jayden felt like screaming. How was he meant to concentrate on his homework with Seb having another one of his meltdowns? He hated him so much sometimes.

Jayden instantly felt ashamed for having bad thoughts about his brother. He didn't mean to. Of course he loved him – it was brother code. You could annoy each other and argue, but deep down you always had to love each other and back each other up –

no matter what. Seb didn't make it easy though. When he was younger, his mum and dad excused it as toddler tantrums, but he was six now and the outbursts were getting worse, not better.

Getting up angrily from his chair, Jayden threw himself down on the bed and pulled a pillow over his ears to drown out his brother's screams.

Shut up, shut up, shut up! he repeated silently to himself, feeling a throb of pain in his forehead.

The screams reached a higher decibel, indicating that someone had opened the bedroom door. Jayden felt his mum touch him on the shoulder. As he edged his face out from under the pillow that was a pretty poor substitute for ear defenders, he saw the look of desperation on her face.

'Please can you help me with your brother, Jayden? You always seem to calm him down better than I can.'

Letting out a puff of breath, he sat up. His

homework would just have to wait.

When Jayden got downstairs, he realised the full impact of Seb's latest meltdown. Various bits of uniform were scattered around the room where he had obviously flung them off in a rage. His school books were in a wet, messy pile next to the wall with his water bottle lying broken next to them. Crouched under the table with a caged animal look about him, Seb stopped screaming when he saw his big brother and then started to cry.

'Mum's making me do my spellings and I don't want to.'

'It's OK, Seb,' Jayden replied in a calm tone. 'I don't like doing my homework either.'

Ducking his head down, Jayden moved underneath the table to sit with his little brother.

'I've got some strawberry laces in my bag,' he said. 'How about I do your spellings with you, and you can eat one every time you write a word?'

Strawberry laces were Jayden's favourite, but he could always ask his mum to get him another packet next time she was at the shop. If Seb stopped screaming, then the sacrifice was worth it. Seb sniffed and wiped his nose on his bare arm. He picked at his toenail, avoiding eye contact.

'OK,' he muttered after a few seconds. 'But I want a strawberry lace before I start.'

Taking this as a win, Jayden climbed out from under the table and ran up to his bedroom to get the sweets. His homework sat unfinished on the desk. He knew that dinner would be ready soon, and by the time he'd helped Seb with his spellings, he'd only have a little while left to do his own work before bedtime. His class were learning about the Titanic at school, and Jayden actually found it really interesting. His mum had even let him watch a movie about it that went on for hours, despite her fast-forwarding a bit in the middle that was supposedly 'inappropriate'. The way a ship that big could just snap in half and crash to the bottom of the ocean fascinated him. Tonight's homework was to write a diary entry as one of the passengers who was lucky enough to be rescued. He'd planned to describe how he would have felt upon realising that the ship was sinking into the deep, icy sea, and how it would have looked as it went up at a vertical angle and then plunged downwards to its fate. He would be too tired to write about that now though, so would just settle for a short paragraph about how lucky he would have felt to be a survivor that night.

'Jayden, have you found those strawberry laces?' his mum called up the stairs.

'Yeah, just coming, Mum,' he said as he closed his bedroom door behind him. Sighing, Jayden expertly detached one of the strawberry laces from the cluster in the bag and put it in his mouth, enjoying the fruity flavour that hit his tastebuds as he wrapped it round his tongue. As he made his way

14

back down the stairs, he thought to himself how his life often felt like it was plunging down, out of control – just like the Titanic. Jumping off the last stair though, he told himself that he would have been one of the survivors that fateful night. He had no choice – his brother needed him.

THE STRANGER

1 WEEK LATER

As the children all piled into the school hall for their morning assembly, they noticed a stranger standing at the front whom they didn't recognise. It was a man dressed in jeans with a dark blue T-shirt hanging over the top of them. Adults probably wouldn't notice this minor detail, but all the children did as not a day went past without one of the teachers bellowing...

'Tuck your shirt in!'

He kept a kind smile on his face as he intermittently nodded to the children who stared at him with curiosity as they shuffled into rows on the cold, hard floor. Cleo felt the breath of the girl behind her puffing on her neck as the teacher instructed their row to move further forward to make room for the Year 6 children.

It was Cleo's first day back after deciding to stay at home last week to help her mum following her fall in the bathroom. Her mum had been diagnosed with a medical condition called multiple sclerosis when Cleo was just five years old. It had sounded like a tongue twister when her mum had first said it. Cleo had felt like her normal-sized tongue had been replaced by a giraffe's tongue as she'd tried to pronounce the words. After five failed attempts, her mum had told her they could call it MS for short. Cleo didn't entirely understand it but knew that it made her mum's muscles feel weak, and her hands and legs didn't work as well as they used to, making walking difficult for her. In the first few years, no-one would really notice that anything was wrong, and Cleo's mum never volunteered the information, so Cleo followed suit, keeping it their little secret. Last year, however, a deterioration in her mum's condition made it necessary for her to use a wheelchair most of the time.

Cleo wriggled uncomfortably as the boy in front of her stretched his arms up to the ceiling and leant back towards her like he was on a sun lounger by a swimming pool.

'Zayan!' bellowed a teacher. 'If you can't sit sensibly, you will sit here with me. If you lean back any further, you'll be sitting on Cleo's lap!'

A ripple of laughter emerged in the hall where it had been silent up until that moment except for the odd cough or hiccup.

'Everyone quiet!' moaned the same teacher who really should have been chuffed at the reaction her joke got instead of telling people off for the laughter she had caused. It wasn't every day a teacher made a comment that was actually funny.

After a quick welcome from the headteacher, Mr Growler, the mystery man introduced himself as Darryl. The use of his first name grabbed the children's attention instantly, confirming their suspicions that he obviously wasn't a teacher as no teacher would *ever* divulge such top-secret information.

Darryl spoke with the confidence of someone who was used to talking to children – unlike a lot of adults who would either bore them to tears with too much information or miss the mark completely by speaking down to them. Darryl seemed to pitch it just right with his warm, friendly tone, and the relaxed way that he perched himself against the edge of the stage with one leg casually crossed over the other.

'I'm here today to tell you about a project that I've set up that will hopefully help a few of you,' he announced, before pausing to gauge the reaction of his audience. 'Can anybody tell me what a young carer is?'

A sea of blank faces gazed up at Darryl until a boy from Year 1 put up his hand and said, 'It's someone young who helps their friend if they fall over and cut their knee.'

'That would be a lovely, kind thing to do,' agreed Darryl.

The boy smiled at him, feeling chuffed that the new visitor had liked his suggestion. A few of the older kids sniggered, knowing that this wasn't the answer that Darryl was looking for, yet not volunteering one themselves.

'Does anyone else have any other ideas as to what it might be?' continued Darryl.

'Is it one of those people who works in old people's homes for a job but they're really young, like about ten?' asked a girl in Year 4.

'Well, I think ten might be a bit young to have a job instead of going to school,' said

Darryl, raising his eyebrows, 'but you're thinking along the right lines. A young carer is a child who looks after someone at home.'

'Like their pet hamster?' a little voice squeaked from the front row.

'Or their cat?' another tiny voice asked.

'Or their gecko?' said the boy next to them, thinking they too had cracked the code. 'I've got a gecko.'

'I've got a snake.'

'I've got a pet dinosaur!'

In the danger of the entire class of Reception children listing every animal that came to mind as they competed for the best pet, Darryl masterfully intervened.

'Taking care of your pets is really important, and I bet you guys are great at it, but I'm talking about taking care of another *person*. Most of you will get to go home after school and maybe have a snack, play some games, watch a bit of TV, do your homework, and then have your dinner cooked for you. Am I right?'

Most of the heads in the school hall nodded as they related to what Darryl was saying. Most of them... but not all.

'Now, just imagine,' continued Darryl, 'if when you go home today, *you* have to make the dinner. What if *you* have to help one of your parents with jobs around the house that they can't do because they have an illness? Not because you're getting pocket money, but because they need you to help run the house and keep everything going.'

Cleo felt her cheeks burn as she heard these words. It was as if Darryl was describing her – but how could he know? She didn't tell anyone at school how much she helped out at home. They wouldn't understand anyway and would probably just call her boring for choosing to look after her mum and make dinner instead of going to the school disco – but to her it wasn't a choice. Her mum needed her, and Cleo had to do all the things that she couldn't.

'Imagine,' continued Darryl, 'if you had a

brother or sister at home who needed extra support and you had to shoulder some of that responsibility?'

Some of the children looked at each other, frowning as if the notion itself was crazy as wasn't that what you had parents for? But a few children sitting in the school hall right at that moment felt a connection. It was as if Darryl had sent a bolt of lightning out of his fingertips that struck them in the chest, sending a tingle down their spine.

'I guarantee you,' said Darryl, 'that there are some young carers sitting here in this room right now.'

With hundreds of eyes fixed upon him, Darryl let a moment of silence fill the hall as he allowed the children to digest his words. Most of them were simply enjoying the break from the monotony of their usual boring assembly, which mainly consisted of moans about trivial matters that only teachers considered important. Several children were listening intently though. Wondering if they could be a child like the ones that Darryl was talking about. And if they were, then maybe there were others like them? Other kids who sometimes felt the weight of the world on their shoulders as they coped with things that most children didn't give a second thought to.

'My job is to visit schools like yours,' Darryl continued. 'To start a group within the school for young carers so that they can all begin to support one another. And the great thing about your school is that you have the perfect place for us to use as our clubhouse.'

Most of the children guessed exactly what Darryl was going to say at this point. He stood there with a smug look on his face, eager to reveal his news, when one of the Year 2 children shouted out, 'The yurt!'

'Yes,' Darryl replied enthusiastically before a teacher could embarrass the child who called out by telling them off for daring to act on impulse. 'The yurt!'

Last year, the parents and children of Summercroft School had raised money through cake sales, sponsored readathons, and an exciting, sponsored sleepover in the school hall. The decision was made to use the money to buy a yurt for the school field. A team of experts had built it over the summer holidays, and it was the talk of the school when the children had returned in September. It was like a giant teepee tent with a hard wood floor. Inside, it was furnished with colourful beanbags and cushions. It was used for after school yoga and for reading groups. The children felt a wave of calm come over them whenever they went in there, as the tranquillity of it was contagious. And now it was also about to become a clubhouse for the young carers of Summercroft School.

'I will be in the yurt this break time and lunch time and, if you think you might be in a situation like I described this morning, then I would love for you to pop in for a chat.

25

I will even have some ginger nut biscuits with me that I might share with you.'

There was an excited 'ooh, yum' from some children as they heard the word 'biscuit'.

'Thank you very much, Darryl,' interrupted Mr Growler as he walked to the front of the hall. 'And remember, children, you only go to see Darryl if you think you are a young carer, not because you fancy a free biscuit!'

One of the teachers, Miss Keir, let out an over-the-top laugh as if this was the funniest joke she'd ever heard. A few of the children screwed up their faces, looking disgruntled that they weren't going to be allowed access to the treat. Cleo had already made her decision without the added temptation of a biscuit though. There was no doubt in her mind that she genuinely qualified with all that she did for her mum, and if there were other kids in the school who were in a similar position, then she wanted to meet them. The weight of loneliness that she always carried in her chest shifted a little as she allowed herself this glimmer of hope.

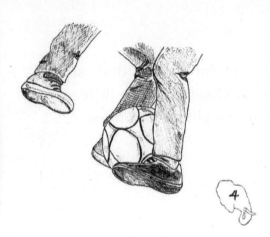

SOGGY CORNFLAKES
AND DOUBT

As the children lined up to make their way back to their classrooms, Jayden thought about what Darryl had said. He often made Seb breakfast in the mornings, as his brother said that he put the perfect amount of milk on his cornflakes, whereas Mum always poured far too much on, making them soggy. And his mum was always asking for his help to calm Seb down when he had one of his meltdowns. He wondered if that classed him as one of the children that Darryl had spoken about.

'Jayden,' whispered his friend Callum, interrupting his thoughts. 'I've brought my football in so we can use it in that match against the Year 3's at break.'

Jayden and Callum were in Year 4 and wouldn't usually entertain the thought of playing football against the kids in the year below them. They preferred to dominate the football pitch themselves, but a new boy had joined Year 3 a few months ago. Everyone called him Pocket Rocket as despite his small size, he was ridiculously fast at running and had quickly won himself a reputation for being a fantastic footballer. With an incredible amount of confidence for a seven-year-old, he had challenged the Year 4 boys to a game of football. Callum had laughed at him when he had proposed the match the previous week. In fact, his exact words were, *'Run along back to the other little toddlers and play with your toys.'* Unphased by this attempt to ridicule him, Pocket Rocket had pretended to walk away and then charged back at an unsuspecting Callum who was about to kick his football back into play. He had performed his legendary slide tackle on Callum to the sound of the Year 4 kids mocking the older boy. Feeling humiliated, Callum had shouted to him that it was a lucky tackle and he'd thrash him in a real game. This had consequently led to a match that Jayden had completely forgotten was going to take place this break time. He wouldn't be able to miss it to go to the meeting in the yurt. He thought to himself how Callum and the other boys from his class would make fun of him for choosing to do that instead of play football. Besides, he decided, he probably wasn't even meant to be there anyway as his mum was always there when he got home from school and made him his dinner. Ginger nut biscuits were his favourite, but he made the decision in that split second that he would play football at break time instead. There was always lunch time if he changed his mind.

THE YURT AND
THE BISCUIT SNATCHER

As Cleo peered hesitantly into the yurt, she felt the warmth of the air within it and the smell of new fabric hit her nostrils. She was wrapped up in her parka coat as the March winds were making the winter cold linger into spring. However, the clear skies had allowed the sun to shine down on the corner of the school field where the yurt had taken pride of place. Like all tents, the material had welcomed the heat of the sun's rays to penetrate it and trap it within, creating a refuge from the windchill outside.

Barely able to concentrate on the fractions work that the teacher had set them for the morning, Cleo had counted down the minutes on the classroom clock until she could head down to the yurt at break time. She always enjoyed going down there for her guided reading sessions and could easily curl up on the yellow beanbag and stay there with a book for the entire afternoon. She loved getting lost in the pages of a book as she escaped her own tiny world which consisted solely of her house and school. In a book she could go anywhere – rainforests, beaches, mountains. The possibilities were endless.

There were lots of other beanbags in different colours, but the yellow one was Cleo's favourite. It reminded her of sunshine and daffodils and baby chicks. Spotting it tucked cosily in the far corner, Cleo thought for a second how it also reminded her of bananas, which she couldn't bear to eat as the texture of them made her gag. Especially the ones with black marks on them where they had sat in the fruit bowl for too long. Cleo felt her jaw tighten and the saliva in her mouth increase as she remembered once sinking her teeth into a banana that had felt furry on her tongue. Pushing the memory to one side, she tried to picture her tiny front garden that was full of daffodils last spring and let the happy yellow thoughts shine through instead.

Darryl was standing next to a small trestle table, emptying on a plate the packet of ginger nut biscuits that he had promised the children. Cleo wasn't too keen on ginger nuts and had hoped that he'd have another type of biscuit there too - maybe chocolate chip cookies – but, knowing that this was probably wishful thinking, she had told herself that a plain digestive was probably more likely. She couldn't believe her luck when she saw Darryl grab a packet of milk chocolate digestives out of a bag and pour them onto a second plate.

Sensing someone watching him, Darryl turned around and gave Cleo a big, welcoming smile.

'Hi,' he said. 'Come on in. I need some help eating these biscuits.'

Feeling a little awkward to be the first one there, Cleo hesitantly walked in and chose a biscuit from the plate that Darryl offered her. Bypassing the two closest to her, she opted for the one in the middle of the plate. Tilted slightly against the other biscuits, she felt like it was calling to her, begging her to fulfil its destiny to melt its chocolatey surface against the tongue of a child who would appreciate it. It would be wasted in the mouth of an adult who could eat any biscuit they liked whenever they felt like it. This biscuit needed to be enjoyed by a child who would savour every bite.

As Darryl was distracted by another child entering the yurt, Cleo claimed the yellow beanbag, being careful not to drop crumbs on it. She discreetly listened to Darryl talking to the girl she recognised from the year above, who too looked a little nervous and unsure. Darryl welcomed her in as warmly as he had Cleo, giving her no time to ponder whether she should be there or not. Taking one of the gingernuts, the girl followed Cleo's lead and sat down on a purple beanbag, giving Cleo a little shy smile before tucking into her biscuit.

Moments later, a boy from Year 3 walked in, full of confidence. Cleo recognised him as Ben Collins' brother. She didn't know his real name but had heard the other boys referring to him as Pocket Rocket. Before Darryl could even offer him a biscuit, the boy grabbed a handful from each plate and ran out of the yurt shouting, 'Sorry, just remembered I've got a football match to play. Thanks for the biscuits though!'

'But these are for the young carers,' Darryl called after him.

Pocket Rocket didn't break his stride as he shouted over his shoulder, 'I caringly poured my left-over rice crispies into my little brother's bowl this morning!'

Cleo couldn't stifle her shocked burst of laughter as she saw Darryl standing there speechless, holding the now near-empty plates in his hands.

'That boy is fast!' he exclaimed, turning round to Cleo and the other girl.

If Pocket Rocket had done that to any of the teachers, they would be chasing after him, demanding that he hand the biscuits back. An image unwittingly flashed into Cleo's head of a teacher standing with their hands on their hips, glaring down at Pocket Rocket as he licked the top of every biscuit to ensure no-one else would want to eat them. Darryl, however, just looked amused. 'Shall we just assume he didn't quite comprehend what a young carer was, and he is going to *caringly* share those biscuits with the rest of his football team?' he asked.

Cleo and the other girl giggled, feeling their nerves ease as Darryl's relaxed manner filled the yurt.

'I think I can see someone else heading this way,' he said as he gazed out of the opening. 'We'll just wait for them and then we'll all have a chat.'

Seconds later, he stood aside to welcome in the third member of the newly formed club, which was yet to have a name.

'Hi,' the boy said, not noticing the girls on the beanbags at first. 'I'm Ethan.'

ETHAN

TWO DAYS EARLIER

'Ethan, honey, can you get the door please? I'm just helping Sasha in the bathroom.'

Ethan heard his mum's voice calling down the stairs. He was winning one-nil in a game of *FIFA* and only had two minutes left until full-time. He had heard the doorbell ring a few minutes before but had ignored it, hoping that someone else would answer it.

'Ethan! Can you hear me?'

He knew that he shouldn't pretend to not hear his mum, but this was important. He was playing against Ben, a boy who had joined his class a few months ago... and he was winning!

The doorbell rang again.

Just one more minute.

Ethan blocked out the noise of the doorbell and his mum shouting down to him. Ben must have heard over the headset though.

'Do you need to go?' he asked. 'You've pretty much beaten me anyway.'

'It's fine,' Ethan replied. He wanted the credit for winning this fair and square.

30 seconds to go.

Ethan moved his star player towards the goal and took a shot.

'GOOOOOOAL!' he shouted down the mic as the ball blasted into the top left corner.

'Nice one,' replied Ben, good naturedly.

The doorbell rang again, more insistently this time.

'Sorry, Ben, gotta go. Good game though. Maybe I'll be online later.'

Ethan ran to the door just as he heard the toilet flushing upstairs.

As he opened it, he was met with the familiar sight of Louisa, the social worker. Standing next to her was a boy who looked to be a few years younger than Ethan, judging by his height. Ethan couldn't tell from his face as the boy was gazing down intently at his feet, avoiding eye contact. Ethan looked down too just in case there was actually something interesting down there that he had missed. *Nope,* he thought to himself, *unless the boy's fascinated by a few ants, there's definitely not something of interest down there.*

'Hi, Ethan,' Louisa said, a touch too enthusiastically for someone who'd been kept on the doorstep for five minutes. 'I was beginning to think you'd all gone out.'

'No, sorry, Mum was upstairs helping Sasha in the toilet, and I was, um, out the back... in the garden... cleaning up dog poo... with a dog poo bag.'

Ethan winced, realising he was doing that thing where you tell a little lie and give far too much detail, giving yourself away.

'Well, better than clearing it up with just your hands,' laughed Louisa in an attempt to be funny in a misjudged child-humour sort of way.

Ethan gave a polite little chuckle which felt less awkward than standing there in silence looking at the top of the boy's head.

'Did your mum tell you I was coming round?' Louisa asked Ethan once she had finished laughing at her own joke.

Ethan's mum was a foster carer. After his dad had died, four years ago, Ethan's mum had decided that she wanted to do something meaningful with her life and had opened the doors of their five-bedroom house along with her heart. Ethan had seen a total of seventeen children come and go in their lives over the past few years. It was so normal to him that he didn't even remember it not being normal. He had his own bedroom, as did his fifteen-year-old sister Ella, but the two spare rooms had become temporary accommodation to children who needed them. Sasha was a three-year-old girl who had been with them for two months, and the remaining room had been empty since a boy called Reuben had been taken in by his grandmother. It would seem that this new boy on the doorstep was about to take Reuben's place and join their family for a while.

'Sorry, Louisa,' said Ethan's mum, rushing to the front door before he had a chance to respond. 'Sasha needed help in the toilet.'

A little girl appeared, popping her head through the gap between Ethan and his mum.

'Hello,' she said, looking up at the boy

inquisitively. She was the perfect height to lock eye contact with him as he kept his head ducked down. 'My foster-mummy told me you're coming to live here, just like I did!'

When Sasha didn't get a response, she decided that the boy needed a hug. Wrapping her arms around his legs she hugged him like she was welcoming a long-lost relative home. 'You can be my brudder too, like Ethan!'

Ethan laughed as the boy squirmed, not sure how to take the news that he had suddenly acquired an annoying little sister.

Deciding to save him, Ethan reached down and picked up Sasha. She stretched up and put her arms around his neck before proudly exclaiming, 'See, he's my brudder.'

Ethan and his mum stepped aside to welcome Louisa and the boy into the house. Ethan's mum had received a call from Louisa that morning asking if they would be able to take in a boy whose parents weren't able to look after him anymore. Ethan didn't know the reason why, and he didn't ask. He just accepted that not all kids were lucky enough to have a mum as great as his, and he had to share his mum with them.

'Do you like *FIFA*?' he asked the boy who still hadn't lifted his head up to meet their eyes yet. When the boy didn't respond, Ethan held out a gaming controller. 'I can teach you if you haven't played before. I've got an Xbox in the lounge.'

The boy seemed to like the sound of that as he lifted his head slightly and took the controller from Ethan. As Sasha followed the two boys into the lounge to tell her *new brudder* lots of information he really didn't need to know about her doll called Maggie – such as how many times a day she had to change Maggie's nappy and how Maggie had fallen down the stairs yesterday when she had tried to walk – Ethan affectionately ruffled Sasha's hair and gave her a remote without batteries in.

'You can play too, Sasha,' he said.

Sasha couldn't believe her luck as she started tapping away at the buttons, thinking that she was scoring goals with the big boys, whilst Ethan's mum made Louisa a cup of tea and got the low-down on the newest temporary member of their family.

PUTTING ON YOUR
'GAME FACE'

'I guess it's just us then,' said Darryl, looking at the three pairs of eyes gazing at him with curious expectation. 'Before I find out your reasons for coming to this fabulous yurt, I'm going to tell you something personal about myself.'

The children sat on their beanbags, staring intently at Darryl, wondering what he was about to divulge to them. Rather than perching on the chair that all the teachers sat on to tower over the children, he had strategically positioned himself on a beanbag just like them – a green one with daisies on it that the girls in Reception all fought over when it was their turn for guided reading in the yurt. Cleo thought it suited him. In the summer term, she would sit on the school field making daisy chains at lunch time. She loved how relaxed this made her feel, and Darryl had an aura about him that invoked that same feeling of relaxation in the yurt.

'When I was a kid,' continued Darryl, 'I was a carer for my parents, who were both partially blind. To me, it was normal to be their eyes, and I would do things that other kids wouldn't even think of.

'What kind of things?' asked Cleo, thinking of everything that she did at home.

'So, for example, whilst other kids were having their hands held tight by their parents to prevent them from running into the road, *I* would be the one holding onto my parents' hands to guide *them* away from the road. Also, instead of being nagged to keep my bedroom clean, it was up to me to keep the whole house tidy so that my parents didn't trip over things. I knew no different, and to me that was just normal life and that was OK. But – and this is a very big *but* – there were times when I felt very alone and like I had the weight of the world on me as I had so much responsibility. I thought all other kids were growing up without a care in the world, and I was the only person who felt like I'd been born a grown-up. But then, when I became an *actual* adult, I realised that there are quite a lot more of us carers out there than I ever thought possible. The problem is, we tend to keep our private life private, and show the rest of the world our game face.'

'What's a game face?' interrupted Ethan.

'A game face is the face that displays the smile that says *everything is OK* but doesn't always quite reach our eyes. Basically, with you guys, it's the face that has the fresh skin of childhood, creating a mask over a mind that is wise beyond its years.'

The children all sat transfixed as they absorbed Darryl's words, suddenly acutely aware that they all felt this way. It was a moment of clarity for all of them as this stranger described the feelings that, before now, had just been unexplained agitations in their heads.

Darryl smiled and rubbed the stubble on his chin as he remembered something from his childhood. 'Of course, I did love the fact that I could put a triple scoop of ice-cream on my cone whilst my parents thought I had sensibly served myself just one! That made all the hard times worthwhile!'

Ethan felt his mouth watering as he imagined three huge scoops of salted caramel ice-cream dripping down a wafer cone. Darryl's voice snapped him out of his daydream just before a bit of dribble started to run down his chin.

'So, I decided to set up these groups in schools to give kids in similar situations to mine the opportunity to realise that they aren't alone in this complicated world, and to hopefully build some friendships and all support each other. How does that sound to you guys?'

Cleo and the other girl nodded their heads whilst Ethan put his hand up.

'I'm not sure I should actually be here.'

'OK,' replied Darryl. 'How about you tell me what made you come here today, and I'll let you know whether I think you were right to come or whether I think you were just out to steal my biscuits.'

'OK, well, um, my mum does stuff for me just like other kids' mums do. She cooks me dinner. She cleans the house. She helps everyone, really.'

'And by everyone, you mean, you... your dad... your brothers, sisters?'

Ethan hesitated for a second, but Darryl's

kind face urged him to continue.

'Well, my dad died when I was younger so, no, not him. But me and my sister, and Sasha, and the boy who came at the weekend. And anyone else who we look after for a bit.'

Some people would have wondered what Ethan was talking about, but Darryl had had a lot of experience of filling in the gaps when children told him half a story.

'So, your mum is a foster carer?' he asked Ethan.

'Yeah, so I'm not really like the kids you were talking about. I just got a bit confused. I'm sorry, I'll leave you guys to it.'

'Just give me two secs before you go,' Darryl said holding up his hand.

Ethan sank back down into the bean bag that he had started to rise from awkwardly – as no-one can ever get up from a beanbag without resembling a baby hippo stuck in a mud pit!

'So, how many foster brothers and sisters

have you had over the years?'

'I don't know, maybe seventeen.'

'That's a lot of kids to be sharing your mum with.'

'Yeah, she's great with them though. Always says she's got lots of love to share around.'

'She sounds like an amazing lady. And what about you? Do you do anything to help them settle in?'

'Well, when Sasha came to us a few months ago – she's the little girl who's three – she was really scared about going to bed in a strange house, so I gave her my *Avengers* glow-in-the-dark torch and told her they'd protect her. I know, it's really stupid, but it calmed her down. And now she calls me her *'brudder'* which is kind of cute. And yesterday, I gave her this remote with no batteries in it to trick her into thinking she was playing on the Xbox with me, which I know sounds really mean, but she thought she was playing so she was really happy.'

'Sounds like you're brilliant with her.'

'And over the weekend, we were meant to go to the cinema in the afternoon, but Mum got a call from our social worker in the morning to say she had a boy who urgently needed to be placed. So, we stayed at home and waited for him instead.'

'That must be tough, having to miss out on your plans for a kid you've never even met before.'

'Nah, it's OK. I'm used to it. It's just the way it is, and these kids need my mum's help, which is more important than some trip to the cinema that we can do another weekend.'

'That's a really great attitude you've got there, Ethan. Your mum must be very proud of you. How did the boy settle in over the weekend?'

'He was a bit shy, but I taught him how to play *FIFA* and he was actually really good at it after a few hours, and even started talking to me a little bit. I know that he's got autism, as I overheard the social worker telling my mum, so I'll probably just need to be patient with him for a while. It's not unusual for the kids who come to have some extra needs.'

'You know something, Ethan?'

'Yeah?'

'You're going to need to get yourself another biscuit because, in my book, you are definitely, without doubt, worthy of being here, and you sound like you're doing an outstanding job at home.'

Ethan smiled up at Darryl and accepted the gingernut that he was being offered. He had just displayed the prime example of a child who was so used to looking out for others that he didn't even realise he was doing it.

'Well, now that Ethan has told us a bit about himself, I think it's only fair that we let one of you talk for a while,' Darryl said, looking at Cleo and the other girl.

Cleo sat silent, not feeling quite ready to share her story. The other girl, being slightly older, took the silence as an indication that she should go next. Any signs of her initial shyness had evaporated thanks to Darryl's natural warmth.

'Hi, I'm Tiegan, and I thought it might be a good idea for me to come to this as my gran moved in with us a few months ago and she has dementia.'

UPSET...ANGRY

...HUMILIATED

Jayden stormed out of the school gates at home time and walked past his mum and brother without saying hello. A few of the other kids pointed at him as they noticed his angry face, laughing at how scrunched up his eyes had gone. Jayden ignored them as he bumped his way through the crowds of parents.

'Jayden, what on earth's the matter?' asked his mum as she caught up with him at their car, where Jayden had come to an abrupt halt.

'Nothing,' he snapped, refusing to look at her.

Hearing the familiar unlocking sound as his mum pressed the button on her car keys, he yanked open the door and climbed into the back seat. His mum knew that she'd get nothing out of him when he was in one of these moods, so chose to let him brood in silence until he was ready to talk. As the engine started up, Jayden felt the burn in his eyes where tears of anger were threatening to flood out after keeping them under control all afternoon.

Gazing out of the window, his vision blurred as he failed to stop the tears from finally falling. It had taken all his strength to hold them in so that his classmates didn't see how upset he was. Upset... angry... humiliated. Definitely humiliated. His teacher's words repeated over and over in his head, like her monotonous voice had implanted itself in his brain.

'It's not good enough, Jayden. Plain lazy, that's what it is. Plain lazy... plain lazy... plain lazy...'

Whilst his classmates had been handed back their marked homework with lots of blue ticks and smiley faces drawn at the end, Jayden had been handed his with red pen scrawled across the bottom reading, 'Poor effort!' Not content with simply writing this negative comment, his teacher had decided to make an example of him in front of the entire class. Towering over him at his desk, she had lectured him on being lazy and how she expected him to stay in and re-do the work at lunch time – the lunch time during which Jayden had hoped he would visit Darryl in the yurt after regretting missing his chance at break time.

Sitting at his desk, he had heard every other child in the school having fun on the playground. He had looked at the piece of paper laid in front of him with his handwriting on it. It wasn't the neatest in his class, but he still felt proud of the joined-up letters swirled together in the blue ink that he was now allowed to use since being granted his pen license the year before. A blue ink that was now ruined by the red ink taking up far too much room, looking messy on the page. He had thought how unfair it was that teachers made kids spend so much time practising perfect sized letters when they couldn't even be bothered to write neatly themselves.

As he had sat there alone – except for the disinterested lunch time supervisor who had the pleasure of guarding him – Jayden had thought back to the night when he had done this piece of homework. He'd actually been looking forward to writing it, to let his imagination run free amongst the facts. He had planned to blend his knowledge of the Titanic disaster with his own personal description of how he visualised it would have felt as a passenger. A passenger plunging towards the icy sea like an out-of-control roller coaster running off its tracks. A deep, uninviting sea that resembled a black hole from space as it unapologetically sucked in anything that came near to it. He would have described it like this – if he had had the chance. But he hadn't. His mum had needed his help with his brother that night, and in the ten minutes he'd had left to do his homework before bed, he hadn't had time to express his thoughts in writing. So, he had written a basic paragraph about feeling thankful to survive. He could have written what he had intended to during his lunch time punishment, but the moment had passed. He would have enjoyed writing it at home, but there was no joy in being forced to write whilst being kept in at lunch time after being humiliated in front of his classmates. Instead, Jayden had added a paragraph about feeling sorry for all those who had tragically lost their lives that night. He had written just enough to get his teacher off his back and when he'd finished, he had looked out of the window and seen Darryl walking down the path towards the school exit. The image of this flashed in his head as his mum pulled into their driveway.

'Who wants a snack?' his mum asked, forcing a cheery tone as she turned the engine off. 'I've got some of those rocky road bites you like, Jayden.'

'Did you get some flapjacks too?' he asked, knowing that his brother hated the texture of the raisins in a rocky road. Seb liked his food bland, and a flapjack, with its consistent taste and colour, was as adventurous as he got when it came to cake.

'Yep, I certainly did. Plus, some of those delicious brownies we like as well.'

Jayden wiped his eyes on his sleeve before climbing out of the car so that his mum didn't see the tears. He did appreciate his mum's efforts to cheer him up, and he really did like those rocky road bites. Blanking out the image of Darryl from his head, he put his game face on and followed his mum and Seb through the front door. Kicking off his shoes, he firmly told himself that there wasn't anything Darryl or anyone else could do to help him, he just needed to get on with things... just like he always had.

PEACE OF MIND

As Cleo rushed home from school, she couldn't stop thinking about her time in the yurt that morning. She had been fascinated as she'd listened to Ethan talk about his foster brothers and sisters, and she couldn't help but feel envious that he had so many children around him. She often daydreamed about having an older brother or sister to help share the burden at home. Or even a younger one just to be silly with sometimes. Last week, she had overheard Ben Collins from her class telling his friend, Tommy, about how he played a game called stair whizz with his younger brothers. Apparently, they took it in turns to sit in a washing basket and push each other down the stairs before crashing into a pile of pillows and duvets at the bottom. She remembered Ben laughing as he'd told Tommy that he'd pushed his brother, Pocket Rocket, so hard once that he'd flown out of the basket halfway down the stairs and catapulted headfirst into the wall. That bit wasn't exactly ideal, and Cleo was slightly perplexed as to why the two boys found this so hilarious, but it had sounded a lot of fun up until then. Cleo wondered what other crazy things they got up to together. She wanted to do something fun like that, but she didn't have anyone at home to do it with. She loved her mum, but it did feel a bit empty and lonely in their house sometimes.

Before she knew it, Cleo came to the crossing at the main road. She gasped as a car whizzed past her despite the lights turning red. It made her think about what Darryl had said about guiding his parents safely across roads when he was a young child. She shuddered at the thought of what could have happened if another less cautious child had been there instead of her. Cleo's mum had always drummed into her how important it was to make sure that the cars actually came to a stop on both sides of the road and not to just rely on the green man to show you it was safe. No matter how much of a hurry she was in to get home to her mum, she always paid attention at the crossing, as if a car hit her and she ended up in hospital, who would be there to take care of her mum?

Once she was safely across the road, Cleo allowed her mind to wander again as she thought back to Tiegan. When Tiegan had told Darryl that her gran had dementia, Cleo didn't fully understand what she was talking about. But as she listened to her in the safety of the yurt, she recognised it as something she had heard of called Alzheimer's – where people lose their memory and can even forget who their family are. Tiegan had told Darryl that it wasn't safe for her gran to live on her own anymore after she had put her dirty clothes into the oven instead of the washing machine and started a fire. Luckily, a neighbour had smelt the smoke and managed to put the fire out before it could spread, but it meant that her gran couldn't be left alone anymore and so had moved in with Tiegan's family. As they only had a three-bedroom house, Tiegan had had to give her bedroom up to her gran and move into her little sister's room with her.

Cleo laughed to herself as she remembered Tiegan saying how it wasn't all bad though, as whenever she got home from school, her gran would give her a hard boiled sweet to suck. She would then repeat this every ten-minutes when the sweet in her own mouth had been sucked to a miniscule size, forgetting that she had already offered one to her granddaughter. Apparently, Tiegan's mum had bought fifty packets from a wholesaler, thinking they would satiate her gran's sweet tooth for the best part of a year. She had no idea that Tiegan and her gran were getting through a packet a day!

As Cleo put her key into the lock, she pushed open the front door and called out to her mum. She could hear her singing in the kitchen and felt a rush of relief come over her as she realised that her mum was OK. She felt her shoulders lower an inch as the tension she hadn't even noticed in her body subsided.

Darryl had told them that he was going to get a phone that would be kept in the yurt. It would just be a cheap old one that you could only use to make phone calls and text rather than play games. Cleo had heard that phones used to be like that in the olden days – like when her mum was younger – but she'd never actually seen one. Her mum had a phone that she used for things like Facebook and Instagram, and she sometimes let Cleo play *Candy Crush* on it, which she loved. There was something mesmerising about the way the brightly coloured sweets neatly slotted onto each other. Cleo could happily gaze at it for hours. The phone in the yurt wouldn't have *Candy Crush,* but Cleo didn't care as she could use it for something far more amazing than that – she could use it to call her mum to check up on her if she was feeling anxious at school. Darryl had told them that he needed to OK it with the headteacher, but his plan was to get a tiny safe that only he, Cleo, Tiegan, and Ethan would know the code for. He had used Cleo as the example that if she was struggling to concentrate at school because she was worried that her mum needed her, she could go to the yurt at break time or lunch time and call home to check up on her. Cleo loved the idea of being able to do that as six hours was such a long time to be at school without knowing whether her mum had fallen over. Most days she was fine, but the fact that it had happened before whilst Cleo was at school meant that she could never quite shift the fear from her mind. She couldn't wait to tell her mum all about it.

SAFE

True to his word, a safe appeared in the yurt just a few days later. It was no wider than a cereal packet and looked very important as it sat in the middle of the trestle table. Its black metal looked out of place in amongst the colourful décor of beanbags and cushions.

The three children, who felt an underlying kindred spirit connection, despite barely ever speaking to each other, met each other's eyes with disbelief. They couldn't believe that their head teacher had given the go ahead for the mobile phone so quickly.

Last year, the school council had asked him for some giant skipping ropes for the playground, and he had told them to put a proposal in writing to him... which he then put out to a teacher vote... which they then put out to a parent vote... which then led to the children having to raise the money for the ropes through a cake sale. The whole process had taken about two months! Yet, here the children were, just two days after their first meeting in the yurt, with the safe in front of them.

'What are you guys doing in here?' came a voice from the entrance.

The children turned to see the boy they recognised as the *biscuit snatcher* from the other day. He was a few years younger than them, which made his confidence even more astonishing, as he swaggered in unashamedly.

'Any biscuits in here, today?'

'No,' laughed Ethan, recognising him as his friend Ben Collins', brother. 'There aren't any biscuits!'

'What's in the safe?'

The boy wandered over to it and started pressing the buttons which bleeped back at him. As he pulled on the handle, the others were shocked to see it open.

'How did you know the code?' asked Cleo in wonder.

'Just guessed it! 1,2,3,4,5,6,7,8!'

Wow, thought Cleo. *Darryl really needs to come up with a better code than that!*

'Waste of time though,' the boy said shrugging. 'No biscuits in there.'

With that, he ran back out of the yurt like a bolt of lightning. If you blinked, you'd have missed him.

'And that is why they call him Pocket Rocket!' Ethan confirmed as they all stood there looking bemused.

Before anyone could reply, Darryl poked his head into the yurt.

'Hey guys. I gather you've seen our safe has arrived.'

'Yep,' said Cleo. 'But I think you need to change the code as 1,2,3,4,5,6,7,8 is a bit easy to guess.'

'That's just the code it comes with,' chuckled Darryl, walking over. 'We get to programme our own code into it.'

'Ah, that makes sense,' said Tiegan as the penny dropped as to why the *biscuit snatcher* was able to open it so easily.

'So, any ideas for a new code?' asked Darryl.

'How about 22334455?' suggested Cleo.

'Still too easy to guess,' said Ethan.

'99999991?' Tiegan offered.

'Still too easy,' said Cleo.

'How about we do a mix of all our birthdays?' suggested Darryl.

Liking the sound of that idea, they took it in turns to punch the first two numbers of their birthday into the keypad as Darryl pressed the reset button on the safe.

'Perfect,' announced Darryl when the safe gave a happy beep to show the new combination had worked. 'Now, engrave this number in your brains and don't, whatever you do, tell anyone else. It's our secret, OK?'

'What was it again?' asked Ethan, raising his eyebrows and biting his bottom lip in concentration. 'My memory is really bad.'

'25120813,' Tiegan said proudly as she showed off her own memory skills.

'Yeah, I think I'm gonna need to write that down,' said Ethan.

'We could write it in disguise,' suggested Cleo who was also worried that she might forget the number. 'Like pretend it's a maths sum, maybe?'

'Great idea,' agreed Darryl as he grabbed some paper and a pen out of his bag. The others stared over his shoulder as he started writing.

25+1-20+8+13=

'Hang on a minute,' said Ethan. 'I think we can actually write this like a sum with 13 as the answer!'

'You are a whole lot better at maths than me if you can do that!' exclaimed Darryl, handing the pen to Ethan.

Ethan bit down on his lower lip again as he focused his mind. Maths was his favourite subject at school. He worked the sum out in his head as the others watched in awe. When he was sure that he was right, he stopped biting his lip and wrote it down.

$25x1-20+8=13$

'That, young man, is seriously impressive,' said Darryl, holding his hand up for Ethan to high five him. Taking the pen from Ethan, he copied the sum down on another two pieces of paper and handed them to Cleo and Tiegan. Tiegan took it to be polite, even thought she was sure she would remember it.

After giving the children a quick lesson on how to use the phone, Darryl tucked it away into the safe and locked the door.

Cleo felt a jolt of happiness shoot through her as she felt the significance of this connection to home whilst at school. She wouldn't take advantage and use the phone every day, but it would make all the difference knowing that it was there for the days when she felt particularly anxious about leaving her mum at home. Tiegan and Ethan knew that they wouldn't really need it, as their situations were very different to Cleo's, but they still felt excited to be part of the secret. The first steps to creating their little bubble of support had been taken.

'Now that's been sorted out,' Darryl said, indicating for them all to sit down on the bean bags, 'we need to have a chat about something that I need your help with.'

The three children looked at Darryl, intrigued as to what he might need from them.

'I have a sneaky suspicion,' continued Darryl, 'that you aren't the only three children in this school who are young carers. And I need your help to do a bit of detective work and recruit the children who, for whatever reason, didn't feel they could come to the yurt on that day that I met all of you.'

BE A WOMBAT

Ethan arrived home to the sound of shouting in the kitchen. Apprehensively, he opened the front door, recognising the voice that was full of angst. Before he could make his way to the commotion, he was met in the hallway by a pair of extremely angry eyes belonging to the boy who had come to live with them on Saturday. The boy who had barely uttered a word to anyone other than Ethan since he'd arrived. Well, he certainly had a lot to say for himself now. Mainly in a very loud voice, along the lines of, 'You're not my mum!' 'You can't tell me what to do!' and 'I hate it here!'

It wasn't unusual for the kids who came to them to be unsettled in their first week or two. Ethan used to get upset by it, especially when they spoke angrily to his mum. He had thought how ungrateful the children were to behave so badly when his mum had offered them a home. He'd wanted to say as much to one girl who had been rude to his mum on her first night there. It was back when his mum had only been fostering for a few months, and it had still felt strange to Ethan and his sister to have other children in the house. This particular girl was only slightly smaller than his sister, so his mum had offered her some of her old pyjamas to sleep in. They were soft, cosy ones with pink flowers on them. The girl had thrown them back at Ethan's mum, shouting that she didn't want any hand-me-downs, especially not ones with 'stupid girly flowers' on. Seeing the girl treat his mum like this when she was being so kind to her had sent Ethan over the edge, and he had stormed towards the bedroom to tell the girl what he thought of her. But, seeing what was about to happen, his mum had stopped him at the door and calmly taken his hand, telling the girl that she would be back in a moment. Ethan's mum had led him back to his own room and explained how the girl would be feeling in their house, that was home to them but unfamiliar to her. She had told him how strange it must feel leave your own family and suddenly be surrounded by strangers and sleeping in a different bed. She had also confided in him that the girl suffered from anxiety, which was going to make it even harder for her to feel at ease. As Ethan had walked out of his room after their chat, he had heard the sound of the girl crying behind the closed door. It was at that point that he decided he would be like his mum and try to help these children who invaded his home. Rather than seeing them like cuckoos stealing his nest, he vowed to be like the wombats he had heard about on the news when there were devastating bush fires in Australia. The wombats who welcomed other animals into their burrows to lead them to safety. Ethan had vowed to be a wombat.

Deciding to give the boy some space to calm down, Ethan continued to the kitchen where he found his mum sipping a cup of tea.

'Hi, sweetheart,' she said giving him a hug. 'How was your day?'

'OK. What was all that about?'

'Oh, you know, just the usual settling in problems. I asked if he needed any help with his homework, and I think it just triggered an explosion of everything he's been bottling up since he arrived.'

Ethan nodded, unphased by the episode after seeing it countless times with other kids. Sometimes their anger came out most when his mum showed them kindness. A kindness that was alien to some of them if they came from a home where love wasn't readily given. Ethan likened it to when he was having a bad day and was able to hold his feelings in until his mum asked him if he was OK. Mums seem to have a special knack for opening the lock in your brain which keeps your emotions inside. One query of 'are you OK?' from your mum and it all comes cascading out.

'Ethan!' exclaimed a little voice of someone joining them in the kitchen.

Ethan felt a tiny pair of arms hugging him tightly round his legs.

'Are you still my brudder?'

It was a question Sasha asked Ethan at least five times a day, and his response was always as patient as the first time she asked. His mum had told him that after being separated from her own family, Sasha needed reassurance that Ethan wasn't going to leave her too.

'Yep,' he said, picking her up. 'I'm still your brother, and Ella is still your annoying sister too.'

Sasha giggled as he tickled her ribs. 'Can you play with me now?' she asked, looking up at him with her big, innocent eyes.

All Ethan really wanted to do was see if Ben was online on the Xbox so that he could try and beat him again at *FIFA*. He wondered if the gaming controller without batteries trick would work again. That way, Sasha would think he was playing with her, and he would get to play with Ben.

'OK,' he said, putting Sasha down so that he could sneakily remove the batteries from the spare remote. 'You can play Xbox with me for a bit.'

Sasha squealed as she couldn't believe her luck at being allowed to play such a big-boy game again. Knowing what he was up to, Ethan's mum mouthed *thank you* over Sasha's head.

As Ethan turned on his Xbox, he was disappointed to see that Ben wasn't online. He was just about to start playing by himself, when an invite popped up from the username, *JammyJay*. After a few seconds of wondering who this might be, he realised that it was a boy from the year below him at school who he'd played online with a few months ago. He couldn't picture exactly who he was, but remembered that he was friends with someone who had a brother in Year 5 at school. The four of them had formed a squad together in another game they were playing. *JammyJay* must have kept him as an Xbox friend. Ethan wouldn't usually play with someone in Year 4, but none of his other friends seemed to be online, so he accepted the invite and spoke into his mic.

'Hi.'

'Hi. Do you wanna play *FIFA*?'

'Sure.'

The two boys kicked off their game with Sasha furiously pressing buttons next to

Ethan, thinking that every goal the players scored was down to her amazing skill. *JammyJay* actually gave Ethan a really good run for his money, considering he was a year younger. Just as *JammyJay* made a run, threatening to score a belter of a goal, Ethan heard him shouting and his player just stopped. Seizing his opportunity to tackle the player whilst he stood defenceless, Ethan heard *JammyJay* moaning at someone for turning off the TV. *Who would turn it off when he's in the middle of a game?* thought Ethan. It was far too early for his parents to be calling him for dinner. Ethan's mum had been known to come and abruptly turn off the TV when he was mid game. But she only did this after she'd got fed up with him replying, 'In a minute,' after continuously asking him to come to the table. But Ethan hadn't overheard anything from *JammyJay*'s mic asking him to stop playing. As he ran the length of the pitch with none of the opposition coming close, he scored a textbook goal. Next thing he knew, *JammyJay* had left the game.

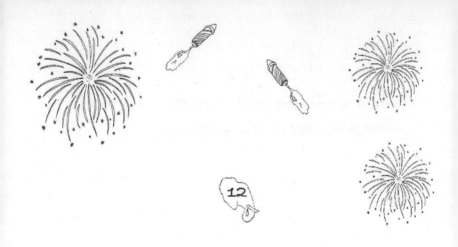

12

FRIENDSHIP

AND FIREWORKS

Cleo and Tiegan sat on their beanbags in the yurt where they had both decided to spend their break time. The other children in the school were envious as they saw the two girls striding over the field towards it. They wished that they too could be part of the secret club that had endless biscuits, and hot chocolate with marshmallows, and candy floss, and cupcakes... At least that was what the rumours going around school were. In reality, they had only had biscuits at their first meeting with Darryl, who was only planning on coming to meet them once a week now that he had set up the club. How often they came together in the yurt was entirely up to them, but Cleo and Tiegan had fallen into a pattern of meeting in there most break times. They had instantly clicked with each other the first time that it was just the two of them in there. Cleo had tripped over the entrance to the yurt as she hadn't realised that the zip was slightly raised. This had broken the ice between them, as Tiegan had laughed so hard as Cleo appeared in a heap on the floor that a noisy fart had slipped out. When the two girls had finally calmed their laughter down, they agreed that the embarrassing outburst would be part of the unwritten code that 'what happens in the yurt, stays in the yurt'. Darryl made it very clear in their first meeting that part of supporting each other meant that they didn't disclose to others anything that they told each other about their personal lives at home. The yurt had fast become their own little sanctuary where they could escape.

The girls looked up as Ethan poked his head in. He hadn't been coming to the yurt as often as they had, but it was cold outside today, and he wasn't really in the mood for playing football with his classmates. He sank onto a beanbag, yawning. Sasha had had a nightmare last night and had woken the whole house up screaming at 4am. Ethan hadn't been able to fall back to sleep and, after a morning of sitting in a stuffy classroom, the tiredness had hit him like a freight train.

'We were just talking about what Darryl said about finding other children who were reluctant to come forward when we did,' said Tiegan. 'Have you found any?'

Ethan shook his head.

'It's hard, isn't it?' said Cleo. 'I mean, us three had no idea about each other, so spotting someone else like us isn't going to be easy.'

'And we're all so different in what we go through at home, so it isn't like anything in particular you can pinpoint,' agreed Ethan.

'Darryl's right though,' said Tiegan. 'There must be others in a big school like this. They probably just don't know they are carers as they're so used to it.'

'Or maybe they're worried about people finding out,' said Cleo.

'Why would they be worried?' asked Ethan, yawning again.

'Well, when my mum got worse, I was worried that someone might take me away from her,' confessed Cleo. It was a fear that she had never told anyone before, and she surprised herself that the words came so freely to these two children whom she hadn't even been friends with until just a few weeks ago. 'And when Darryl popped in a few days ago, do you remember him saying that some children have parents who are really depressed? I'm not sure I'd tell anyone if my mum was like that.'

The children all sat there in silence for a minute.

'What do you mean by depressed?' asked Ethan. He had heard Darryl talking about it but felt a bit embarrassed to ask him what it meant when Cleo and Tiegan seemed to already know.

'You know when someone's feeling really low, and it makes it hard for them to do stuff like they usually would. Sometimes they just want to stay in bed or mope about the house,' Tiegan told him. As the oldest in the group, she was fast adopting the know-it-all big sister role.

'Well, I guess if they don't want to come to us, then we need to look for the signs that Darryl told us about,' said Ethan.

'Oh yeah, like being late to school all the time or having lots of days off sick,' said Cleo.

'Yep, just what I was thinking,' agreed Tiegan, not wanting to be out done by the children younger than her. 'And not doing their homework.'

'Or not doing the extra stuff at school like the school disco,' said Cleo, referring to her own experience.

'Or being really secretive and not wanting to join in with everyone at break time,' suggested Ethan.

Tiegan racked her brain trying to think of the other signs that Darryl had told them to look out for. But before she could think of anything, Cleo spoke again.

'Or sometimes they're really naughty in class because they're feeling frustrated or angry.'

'Or they, um, um, um...' Tiegan desperately tried to add something.

Ethan interrupted Tiegan's umming. 'I think I know someone.'

'Who?' they both asked.

'There's this boy in Year 3 that I heard some other kids being mean to in the playground the other day. Apparently, he goes to sleep in his school clothes to make it quicker getting ready in the morning.'

'That doesn't mean he's a young carer, Ethan,' chastised Tiegan. 'He could just be trying out more efficient ways of getting to school on time.'

'Maybe,' agreed Cleo. 'But most parents would make their kids get out of their school clothes and put pyjamas on after having a bath or something, wouldn't they?'

'Yeah, but boys don't like washing,' announced Tiegan, like she was the expert of all things boy-related. 'They like staying grubby.'

Ethan looked offended. 'I had a shower, last night,' he announced. He didn't tell them that his last shower before that had been four days ago. 'Girls can be just as smelly you know!'

Before they could get into a full scale *girls versus boys* argument, Darryl appeared.

'We didn't know you were coming back so soon,' said Tiegan, speaking for the group.

'I wasn't planning to,' said Darryl. 'But I got a call from the school yesterday about a child they thought might need our help, so I've popped in to see them.'

'Who is it?' asked Ethan.

'I can't really tell you, but if it turns out they want to be part of our group, you'll meet them soon enough. They're a bit younger than you guys though.'

'The kid in Year 3,' Tiegan said smugly, like she knew exactly who it was.

'That was my guess!' said Ethan, not wanting to miss out on getting the credit for his detective work.

'Could be,' said Darryl, giving nothing away. 'So, tell me, how are things with all you guys?'

'Good.'

'OK.'

'Not bad.'

'How's your gran, Tiegan?' Darryl asked, when all the children had offered him the standard answers children give you when asked how they are. 'Still giving you those sweets every day?'

'Yep,' Tiegan giggled. 'She thought I was her sister yesterday though, which was kind of sad and funny all at the same time.'

'That must have felt strange,' said Darryl. 'Did she think that she was a young girl?'

'Yeah, she wanted me to do bunches in her hair, which is what made it so funny. Bunches aren't a good look for a seventy-year-old lady with thinning, grey hair and a wrinkly neck!'

As they all laughed, Tiegan felt a pang of guilt. 'Isn't it bad that we're all laughing about it?' she asked.

'Sometimes we need to laugh, Tiegan,' said Darryl. 'When you're living the lives that you guys are, sadness and laughter will often be entwined, and that's OK. That's one of the reasons it's good to form a support group like you guys have now. You kind of get what each other goes through. And you know you can freely talk about it with each other as we made the pact about not telling anyone else what we tell each other in here, remember?'

Tiegan blushed slightly, feeling grateful that this pact had saved her from the entire school knowing that she had farted when she'd laughed. If she was being honest, it wasn't the first time that it had happened.

Cleo and Ethan nodded their agreement, feeling strangely comfortable in the knowledge that they could all confide in one another after bottling up certain things inside all this time.

'And another thing I wanted to talk to you guys about is whether I can do anything to help you,' said Darryl. 'Children who have a lot of responsibility at home often miss out on things that the others take for granted, so if there is something that you think I can help with in any way, then let me know.'

'What kind of thing do you mean?' asked Cleo.

'Like, when I was a kid, I remember

everyone going to an amazing firework display on the school field. I didn't tell my parents about it as knew they wouldn't be able to appreciate all the amazing colours, and they'd just hear the bangs which might have startled them. So, I sat looking out of my bedroom window, straining to catch a glimpse of the show through the trees. Now, every November, I make a point of finding the biggest, brightest display that I can.'

'I never get to go to the school disco,' said Cleo. 'But that's OK,' she quickly added. 'I really don't mind.'

'It could be something really simple that other kids take for granted too,' said Darryl. 'Like getting help with your homework or having breakfast. The point of this group is to chat things through and support each other, so anything you think of, just let me know, OK?'

The children all nodded as they digested what Darryl was saying. Tiegan's mum had been so distracted looking after her gran the other morning that she had forgotten to make Tiegan the toast she had promised, and when she'd remembered, it was too late.

'Maybe, we could keep some breakfast snacks in here,' she tentatively suggested. 'You know... just in case.'

'Great idea,' Darryl said. 'Does everyone like cereal bars?'

***

The children made it back to their classrooms just in time, as the bell went to signal that break time was over. The field where the yurt took pride of place wasn't enormous, so it only took a minute for them to make their way to the playground where all the other children were. But that minute could make the difference between slotting unnoticed into line with the rest of their class or being on the receiving end of *The Teacher Look*! Every child in the world will know *The Look* – some teachers went for a raise of the eyebrows whilst pressing their lips together. Others were able to make their eyes appear twice their normal size, making themselves look somewhat like an ostrich as they glared at you. Whatever style they went for, *The Teacher Look* was unmistakeable. Right at that moment, Cleo was the recipient of the ostrich glare, as she tried to subtly walk into the room. She was at least ten seconds behind Ethan, whose longer legs had allowed him to catch up with the last person. She was tempted to impress her teacher with the fact that ostrich eyes are actually bigger than their brains, but realised that she should probably save that gem for another time.

Once the teacher had finally shrunk her eyes back to normal size, Cleo glanced around her, trying to see if any of her classmates, apart from Ethan, fitted the mould of a young carer. They all looked like they didn't have a care in the world though as the teacher announced the exciting news that the school would be hosting a talent show.

All eyes looked at Ethan as the children remembered the success of the last talent show when he was crowned the winner. He had felt so proud as he'd looked into the audience and met his mum's eyes. She had brought along his sister, Ella, and the two children that they were fostering at the time. At £5 a ticket he had been worried that his mum might not be able to come, but she had said that she wouldn't miss it for the world. His winning act had been chosen by a group of judges, which consisted of a boy and a girl from each class. They had been unanimous in their decision to award first prize to him as he'd delighted the audience with his comedy act – which consisted mainly of him roasting the teachers! Luckily, the majority of them took it good naturedly –apart from Mr Growler, the head teacher, whom the children had never seen crack a smile. He had looked like he was about to explode when Ethan had told his joke, *'Mr Growler, what do you call headlice on the head of a bald man?'* looking pointedly, and some would say bravely, at his head teacher, who had a distinct lack of hair. The entire room had erupted into laughter as he delivered the punch line: *'Homeless!'* The most rewarding laugh though came from his foster brother, William, who usually hid behind a scowl. Ethan recalled this as being the night that William let his guard down and allowed himself a moment of carefree happiness like all the other children. The significance of that had meant even more to Ethan than winning the competition.

Cleo gazed out of the window, daydreaming of the act that she would have done, had she lived the life of a normal child. An act where she would perform tricks with her dog, wowing the audience with their perfectly executed hoop jumps and seesaw walks. She imagined her dog licking her all over her beaming face as the head teacher announced them as the winners! Sighing, she allowed the vision of her imaginary dog to fade from her mind as she brought her attention back to her lesson.

TOLERANCE

That night, Cleo couldn't stop thinking about other children who may need to be part of their group. She had been known to obsess over things – once she got something in her head, she found it hard to let go. Switching on her bedside lamp, she grabbed the notepad and pen that she always kept next to it. Running her fingertips over the sequins that covered the notepad, she watched them shimmer as they reflected the light. Her mum had once told her that it sometimes helped to write things down if they were stopping you from sleeping. That way, you could get them out of your head and allow your brain to relax.

The soft glow of her lamp created shadows on her yellow walls. It didn't scare her though. Laying the notepad on her lap, she held her hand up, pressing her pinky finger and the one next to it into her thumb to create a hole. Then, wiggling her other two fingers up and down, she smiled as the image of a rabbit appeared on her ceiling. She had a vague memory of her dad making shadow shapes on the ceiling for her when she was little. Her favourite was the flying bird, but no matter how much she tried to master it, hers always looked more like two pieces of wilted cabbage flopping around. She rarely thought about her dad now. He and Cleo's mum had separated shortly after her mum became ill. She'd seen him most weekends to start with, but then he got a new job which meant he moved to America.

Then came the new wife... and then the new children. He had said that Cleo could go to visit them whenever she wanted to in the school holidays, but she knew that she couldn't leave her mum on her own. She didn't like leaving her whilst she was at school, let alone leaving her to fly somewhere thousands of miles away.

Picking up the pen, Cleo wrote the first thing that she needed to get out of her head, just like her mum had told her to do.

Number 1 – Call Dad and ask him how to perfect the flying bird shadow shape.

She then put a big cross through what she had just written and started scribbling over it for good measure before writing her next thought down.

Number 2 – Don't call Dad. He's the

stupid grown-up who left. He should call me!

She then put a cross through this, a scribble, and a huge exclamation mark for finality.

Number 3 — Grown-ups make mistakes too. Me and mum are fine. Don't hold a grudge.

Cleo sighed as she re-read what she had written. It looked like something far too wise for her young ten years, but she had had no choice but to grow up quickly. Looking after her mum had taught her to be resilient and tough. She had a degree of tolerance towards others that many children of her age lacked. She often saw other kids in her class bickering over things that seemed so trivial to her. Like two girls, Lottie and Emily, whom she had overheard arguing about who had the best flavour of Monster Munch in their lunch box. Lottie was adamant that pickled onion was the best whereas Emily was having none of it and considered the beef ones to be the superior flavour. Instances such as this paled in comparison to Cleo's tolerance of her dad and his dreadful inability to make good choices in life. She could understand his decision to split up with her mum, as it wasn't unusual for parents to get divorced sometimes, but the decision to move to America was definitely up there with one of his worst choices – in Cleo's wise opinion anyway.

Satisfied that number three could stay on the page and didn't need crossing out, Cleo then moved onto the most important matter that was keeping her awake.

Number 4 – How to find other young carers.

She paused and absent-mindedly put the end of the pen between her teeth as she tried to think what to write next. She remembered an author coming to their school last year and telling them that no idea was a bad idea. Every idea should be written down, as it could then lead you on to another idea that might be perfect. She had, of course, been referring to ideas for creating stories, but Cleo could adopt the same method for her plan. Closing her eyes, she tried to focus. She then started writing anything that came into her head.

1 – Walk around the playground asking everyone if they look after someone at home.

2– Borrow a megaphone and stand at the yurt shouting 'Any young carers here?'

3 – Make a poster.

Looking over her three ideas, she then wrote corresponding comments as to how successful she thought those methods would be, followed by a big tick or a cross.

1 – Risk of younger kids telling me all about their pets... Risk of older kids making me feel awkward for talking to them... Risk of being hit in the face by a football. X

2 – Risk of looking like a fool. Does anyone even use megaphones anymore?! X

3 – Risk of favourite colour felt-tips running out. Don't worry – can ask for more for my birthday. ✓

Cleo looked over the page in her notepad that had been blank just moments before. *That actually worked,* she thought to herself. Placing her notepad and pen back on her bedside table, she turned off her lamp and snuggled under her warm duvet. Smiling to herself, she began to think about the colours that she would use on her poster and, with swirls of purples, blues, and of course yellows, filling her eyelids, she drifted off into a deep sleep.

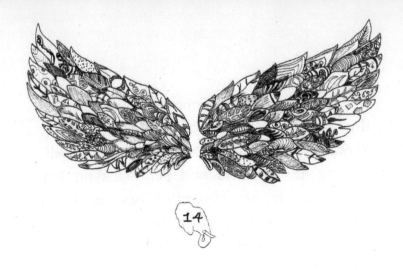

THE ART OF
DIPLOMACY

'Shall I do one of those too?' Ethan asked, walking into the yurt at break time the next day.

Cleo and Tiegan were leaning on the table, creating posters with their neatest possible bubble writing.

'I quite like doing bubble writing.'

'Sure,' replied Cleo, handing him a piece of plain white paper. 'Help yourself to any of these pens.'

As she said this, she sneakily slid the yellow pen underneath her hand. She didn't want her favourite colour to run out on someone else's poster.

Inspired by her late-night idea, Cleo had rushed to the yurt at the first chance possible to fill in Tiegan on her plan to put posters up around the school. Fully embracing the idea, Tiegan had joined Cleo and together they had set to work and created four eye-catching posters. With Ethan's, that would make a total of five to be strategically positioned where children would see them.

'So, where are we going to put these?' asked Ethan.

'I thought maybe one in the library,' suggested Cleo. 'And one in the hall so people see it when they're queuing up for lunch or assembly.'

'We should put one in the toilets too,' Tiegan advised.

'Two in the toilets,' added Ethan. 'One in

the boys' and one in the girls'.'

'Where shall we put the last one?' asked Cleo.

'How about just underneath the feather collage?' suggested Tiegan. 'Everyone loves looking at that.'

She was referring to the giant wing collage that was made up of hundreds of pieces of card cut into the shape of feathers. Each one had been individually decorated by a child at Summercroft School and then placed together to make two giant wings. The sentiment was that if all the children came together and supported one another, they could fly. Obviously, they wouldn't literally be able to fly – it was to symbolise the feeling that together they could achieve anything. But Cleo had always loved it, ever since decorating her feather the previous year.

'That's perfect,' said Cleo smiling. 'As that's kind of what we're like isn't it.'

She blushed a little as she said this, hoping that Tiegan and Ethan would see their tiny group like that too. Ethan saved her blush from growing though as he smiled.

'Yeah, I like that. We support each other like all the feathers.'

'Maybe we should give ourselves a special group name?' suggested Tiegan.

'Like what?' asked Ethan.

'I don't know, like maybe 'The Flying Feathers?'

'Nah,' said Ethan. 'Too cheesy. How about 'The Flyers.'

'That's rubbish,' countered Tiegan.

'What about calling ourselves after an animal?' suggested Cleo. 'What's everyone's favourite animal?'

'Mine's a cat,' said Tiegan.

'Mine's a dog,' said Cleo.

'Mine's an elephant,' said Ethan.

'You can't have an elephant as a pet!' laughed Tiegan.

'She didn't say your favourite pet,' retorted Ethan. 'She said your favourite animal.'

'I did say animal,' agreed Cleo.

'OK, well we can't call ourselves our favourite animal,' said Tiegan. 'As we all have different favourites. Although why a cat isn't everyone's favourite, I do not know.'

'How about we name ourselves after an animal that's known for being caring,' suggested Ethan tentatively. 'You know, because we're young carers, so kind of like a play on words.'

'Dogs are really caring,' said Cleo, still pushing her favourite animal into the mix. 'Did you know that mother dogs have been known to adopt kittens as part of their puppy litter if the kitten's mum can't look after them?'

'Aw, that's so cute,' said Tiegan. 'I'd love a kitten.'

'Let's focus,' said Ethan, seeing the girls getting distracted by images in their heads of puppies and kittens.

'You know elephants are meant to be one of the most caring animals on the planet,' he informed them. 'I saw a documentary about them once which said that they are totally selfless and go out of their way to help others. We could be The Elephant Squad!'

'I actually really like that,' agreed Cleo.

'How about The Elephant Troop,' suggested Tiegan, torn between liking the name and wanting to be the one to come up with the final suggestion.

'Hmm, I prefer The Elephant Squad,' said Ethan. 'How about we let Cleo choose.'

Not wanting to let either of her new friends down, Cleo chose to be diplomatic. 'Let's pick the name out of a hat,' she suggested. 'Only we don't have a hat, so I'll write both names down and put one in each hand. Whichever one you pick is the name we go with. OK?'

'OK,' they agreed.

Cleo ripped a piece of paper in two and wrote The Elephant Squad on one and The Elephant Troop on the other. Folding them up tightly, she put one in each hand and placed her hands behind her back. Taking it very seriously, she swapped the pieces of paper from one hand to the other until even she didn't know which hand contained which name. Feeling very important, she then put her scrunched up hands out in front of her.

'Who's going to pick?' she asked.

'You can if you like,' Ethan said to Tiegan. Years of welcoming in foster children had given him great diplomacy skills. He knew that it didn't really matter who picked the hand as none of them knew which name was in which one, but he also sensed that Tiegan was desperate to be the one to pick.

She studied Cleo's hands for a minute as if she had suddenly developed the superpower of X-ray vision. Pursing her lips together in concentration, she pointed at Cleo's left hand.

'That one!'

As Cleo opened her hand to reveal the folded-up piece of paper inside, Tiegan

118

snatched it and opened it up. Not speaking, she held it up so that Cleo and Ethan could see what was written on it. Judging by the sulky expression on her face, they already knew what it said before they read the words.

Ethan smiled at Cleo, 'I guess we are now officially known as The Elephant Squad.'

NOT MISSING OUT

Cleo looked around her, not quite believing that she was actually here. The school hall was packed full of chairs, which seated children, parents, and even some grandparents. There was a rumble of chatter all around her as excited voices discussed what they were about to see.

After they had decided on their group name the other day, Ethan had asked the rest of The Elephant Squad if they would be going to watch the school talent show. Without thinking, Cleo had given her usual response that she wouldn't be able to go, knowing that her mum would need her at home.

Unlike other children though, Ethan hadn't just accepted her answer. He knew that his mum would be bringing not just him, but also his sister, Ella, his foster sister, Sasha, and the new boy that had recently joined them. He didn't see why Cleo couldn't bring her mum along and told her as much.

At first taken aback by his assumption that she could just get on with it like his mum seemed to, Cleo actually couldn't think of an answer as to why she shouldn't bring her mum along. She had got so used to dealing with everything herself and not mentioning things like this to her mum, that she had just dismissed the talent show from her thoughts, like she had the school disco.

But with Tiegan and Ethan's encouragement, she had agreed to ask her mum if she felt up to coming along to the talent show.

And judging by the look on her mum's face now, as she sat next to Ethan's mum, chatting away like they were old friends, it had definitely been the right thing to do. Tiegan had come along with them too, as her mum had thought that it would be a bit much for her gran to cope with and her dad wouldn't have been home from work in time.

When she had heard this, Cleo hadn't hesitated in inviting Teiegan back to her house after school so that she could walk to the talent show with Cleo and her mum.

Cleo hadn't had a friend over after school in as long as she could remember and, as Tiegan had walked along beside her, matching her fast pace step for step, Cleo had felt a sense of contentment that she hadn't experienced in a long time. It was the secure feeling of having someone with her, which most children took for granted. To Cleo, who never spent time with other children outside of school, it was a big thing. And as they returned to school a few hours later, pushing Cleo's mum in her wheelchair, their friendship felt like the most natural thing in the world.

'It's about to start!' exclaimed Tiegan, nudging Cleo's leg. As the lights dimmed, Sasha excitedly clapped her hands from where she sat next to Cleo on Ethan's lap. Ethan's most recent foster brother, who'd been introduced to them as Adam, sat the other side of him. Cleo had noticed how naturally Ethan tried to include him and, although Adam was very quiet, it made Cleo smile when she saw him laughing at something Ethan had said.

Cleo immediately recognised the boy who confidently strode onto the stage to open the show. He was dressed in an Arsenal football kit with a ball tucked under his arm. There was only one boy in the school who had that unmistakeable swagger to his walk, despite only being in Year 3. It was Pocket Rocket – the *biscuit snatcher* from the yurt!

The crowd started to cheer as Pocket Rocket dazzled them with his football skills. Cleo didn't know much about football, but she could see that he had talent as he perfected his keepy-uppies. Suddenly he kicked the ball as hard as he could towards the audience. Cleo gasped as she felt her hair blow under the breeze of the ball as it narrowly missed the taller man sat in front of her and flew over her head. Seated in the back row so that her mum's wheelchair could sit discreetly behind them, Cleo craned her neck backwards to see the ball drop expertly into the basketball net just behind them. Ethan jumped to his feet cheering and clapping as Tiegan and Cleo followed suit along with the rest of the crowd. Cleo looked to her left to check in with her mum to make sure that she was OK and saw that she was cheering and clapping too from her seat. The atmosphere was electric as Pocket Rocket jumped off the edge of the stage and ran through the gap in the middle of the audience to retrieve his ball. Cleo laughed as she saw him high five everyone he passed, including her mum who held her hand up to him as he neared their row! She looked at Cleo afterwards with the excitement of someone who had just high-fived a famous person. Cleo mirrored her mum's wide eyes and open mouth to join in with her enthusiasm. She hadn't seen her mum have this much fun in ages.

Several predictable acts followed which mainly comprised of children showing off their singing talents. Some of them had pretty good voices, but most of them were obviously under the illusion that they had the voice of an angel when in fact they sounded more like a screeching Tasmanian devil. The audience were saved from the torture when two little boys from Reception ran on stage dressed as super heroes and, without any hint of stage fright, introduced themselves as Mr Magnificent and Awesome Man.

'Oh, my goodness, they're so cute!' exclaimed Tiegan. 'Look at their little homemade costumes!'

'What's it saying on their backs?' Sasha asked Ethan, gazing up at her *big brudder* as she sat on his lap.

'That one there on the right says 'MM', which stands for Mr Magnificent,' he explained patiently, as the music started, 'and that one there on the left says 'AM', which stands for Awesome Man.'

Cleo didn't know what was cuter, the two little boys on stage or Sasha sharing such a lovely bond with Ethan.

The audience started clapping along to the music as the boys began to dance their little hearts out. It was the kind of high energy, care-free dancing that Cleo might have embraced when she was their age – before things got tough. Seeing her mum enjoy every second of their act made her decide to put music on more at home.

Just when Cleo thought there surely couldn't be any acts left, she saw some scaffolding being erected on the stage. As the audience looked on with curiosity, a wooden board was placed on top of it.

'What do you think that's for?' she asked Tiegan.

For once, Tiegan didn't try to be the one with all the answers. 'I actually have no idea,' she admitted, looking as perplexed as everyone else.

Before they had time to speculate further, Ben Collins, Pocket Rocket's big brother, walked casually onto the stage dressed in a karate gi. Taking hold of a stick that had just been launched at him across the stage, he confidently climbed up the scaffolding to stand on top of the wooden board.

'Wow, he's brave,' whispered Cleo. 'I get scared just standing at the top of an escalator.'

Sasha giggled and looked at Cleo. 'You're funny!' she said.

You could have heard a pin drop in the audience, as the murmur of voices hushed as Ben started to move around. The stick became a blur before their eyes as he expertly twirled it around whilst performing kicks and punches to perfection. Cleo heard herself gasp when he got so close to the edge of the board that she thought he might fall. But each time, he placed his feet perfectly, never once losing his balance.

Everyone sat in awed silence as, for his grand finale, he leapt off the scaffolding towards a long piece of wood. Everything turned to chaos, however, as Ben's feet hit the ground and he brought his hand crashing down. Instead of breaking in two, the piece of wood that had been set in front of him stayed intact. As a piercing scream filled the hall, there was no doubt in the audience's mind that he had meant to break the wood. His act had ended in an epic fail.

Cleo watched with concern as she saw a lady rush onto the stage who she presumed must be his mum. Placing an ice pack on his hand which must have been in agony, she walked him off the stage, presumably to go to hospital for an X-ray.

'I don't think he'll be beating me at FIFA any time soon,' said Ethan. 'That looked painful.'

The vibe in the hall had quickly turned from one of celebration to an uncomfortable air of concern. The head teacher, Mr Growler, tried to recover the evening by inviting the last two acts on stage. Cleo felt sorry for them though, as the earlier buzz had disappeared. The evening was quickly wrapped up after that, as the winner was announced and presented with a cheque for £100. Pocket Rocket ran on stage grinning from ear to ear when his name was announced. Obviously momentarily forgetting his brother's pain, he grabbed the cheque from Mr Growler and gave it a big kiss before waving it in the air for everyone to see. Cleo couldn't help but laugh at his attitude. She really wouldn't be surprised to see him make it as a professional footballer one day.

As the crowds around them started to rise from their seats, Cleo waited patiently for some space to help her mum into her wheelchair.

'Glad you came?' asked Ethan, as he picked up Sasha from his lap.

Cleo smiled at him. 'It was so good,' she said. 'Apart from Ben hurting himself, obviously. But at least I'll feel part of it when everyone's talking about it on Monday, instead of just hearing about it second hand.'

Ethan raised his eyebrows and laughed.

'That's really bad of me isn't it!' Cleo exclaimed as she realised how what she'd just said had sounded. 'I didn't mean it like that. It's just that I wasn't there for the secret school tuck shop at the disco, but I was here for this and it's not like I feel like I missed out this time,' she waffled.

'It's OK,' Ethan reassured her. 'I totally get it.'

Cleo relaxed as she realised that Ethan wasn't judging her for her insensitive comment. He'd understood exactly what she had meant.

'OK, well, I guess I'll see you at school on Monday', said Cleo, stepping aside so that Ethan and his family could go past.

'We'll wait with you whilst the crowd dies down,' said Ethan. 'Make sure you get out OK with your mum.'

Cleo felt a sensation go through her body as Ethan said this. It wasn't like a cold shiver or a shock, though. It was the type of feeling where your body is acknowledging something important before your brain has had time to register it. And as her brain caught up, Cleo realised that she felt supported. She had arrived there tonight thinking that she was helping Tiegan by bringing her along. She was leaving tonight with the support of Tiegan, Ethan, and Ethan's family. Her world, that had just been her and her mum for so long, had suddenly grown, and the feeling of loneliness that she had harboured for so long was starting to feel that little bit less.

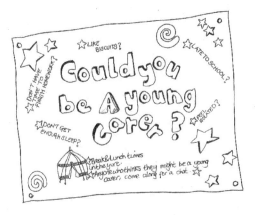

Could you be A young Carer?

LIKE BISCUITS?

DON'T HAVE TIME TO FINISH HOMEWORK?

LATE TO SCHOOL?

DON'T GET ENOUGH SLEEP?

FEEL ISOLATED?

Break & Lunch times in the yurt. Anyone who thinks they might be a young carer, come along for a chat.

16

SEIZE THE OPPORTUNITY

Jayden put his hand up. He'd been trying to ignore the feeling, but it just wouldn't go away. His mum had made him a smoothie for breakfast. He'd rather have had Belgian waffles smothered in Nutella, but his mum had been saying how great it was that he ate whatever she gave him. Knowing that she had had a frustrating morning trying to get his brother to eat, he'd graciously taken the glass from her when she'd offered it. Apart from the suspect green lump that had attached itself to his lip when he'd pulled the glass away, it had tasted surprisingly OK. She'd obviously snuck some spinach in there, thinking he wouldn't notice, but the blend of blueberries, banana, and coconut milk disguised it well. The coconut milk had gone right through him though, and he'd been bursting for a wee all morning.

With a tut, his teacher excused him from the classroom, and he practically ran to the toilets that they shared with Years 5 and 6. Thankful to see that there was no one else in there, he breathed a sigh of relief as he made it to the toilet just in time. As he went to the sink afterwards to wash his hands, he noticed a poster on the wall. It was the bubble writing that caught his eye. The letters alternated between a glittery blue and a striking yellow, and the combination made it stand out against the drab white walls. The paint on the walls was peeling where it had suffered years of water being splashed on it as children flicked their hands dry before reaching for a paper towel.

Seeing the question *'Could you be a young carer?'* in the centre of the poster, reminded him of the man who had come in to talk to the children in assembly about three weeks ago. Jayden had initially regretted his decision not to go to the yurt, but he'd pushed it to the back of his mind and had forgotten all about it. A few of the facts written colourfully around the central question grabbed his attention.

Don't have time to finish homework!
Late to school!
Don't get enough sleep!

It wasn't just that he really liked the style of writing that had been used, it was that he could relate to all those facts. Yawning, he remembered how he had been kept up until nearly midnight last night, as his brother, Seb, had screamed the house down because he couldn't get to sleep. Seb usually had medication to help him, but Jayden's mum had forgotten to pick up the new packet from the chemist before it closed. After his brother was diagnosed with autism at four years old, Jayden understood that Seb didn't experience the world in quite the same way as him, and part of this meant he also struggled to relax his brain when he needed to sleep. Jayden helped Seb whenever he could, but he would be lying if he said he didn't find it tough and draining at times.

There was a smaller section at the bottom of the poster stating that a group of kids met most break and lunch times in the yurt, and anyone who thought they might like to find out more was welcome to go along for a chat. Jayden liked the yurt. Most of the kids at the school did. Its cosy interior and the fact that it was tucked away at the edge of the field made it seem a million miles away from the rest of the school.

Maybe I should go along one day, he

thought to himself. *Just to see what it's like.*

He pondered the thought as he wandered slowly back to his classroom. He was in no rush to get back to the lesson.

'Nice of you to join us again, Jayden,' his teacher barked at him sarcastically as he walked through the door. 'I was just telling the rest of the class about a creative writing session that we have been invited to attend with another school. It's being run by a local author called Leo Sparks, and there are ten spaces being allocated to each class.'

This certainly got Jayden's attention. School work didn't always come easily to him, especially maths, which he'd always struggled with. Writing was his passion. He had notebooks at home which he kept hidden in his sock drawer. In them, he'd written plans for stories that he wanted to write one day. He'd started the first one when he was six and had filled it with ideas about spaceships and talking animals. Nowadays, his ideas were more elaborate, and he'd even written a couple of chapters for his latest story. A creative writing class with an actual, real-life author would be amazing!

'So, if you're interested', continued the teacher. 'Ask your parents to return the form that is being emailed to them today. If there are more than ten of you who are interested, we will randomly draw names from a hat.'

****

When he got home, Jayden couldn't wait to tell his mum about the creative writing session. She loved to hear about his ideas for stories, so he knew she'd be keen for him to attend.

'Of course, JayJay,' she said, using her nickname for him when he told her about it. 'I'll check my email now and see if the form's there.'

'Great, thanks, Mum. Can I play on the

Xbox for a bit?'

'Sure. I'll just go and see what Seb wants and then I'll check for the form.'

Just as she'd been about to search for it, Seb had started shouting from upstairs. Jayden wished that sometimes his mum would just focus on his needs first. It would have taken her only a minute to check her phone for the form. As he switched on the Xbox and made a mental note to remind her to check her email, he typed in his username, *JammyJay*.

'The emails come through JayJay,' he heard his mum shout from upstairs a few minutes later. Jayden smiled to himself, hoping that there would only be a few others in the class who wanted to go. He'd hate to miss out if his name wasn't pulled out of the hat.

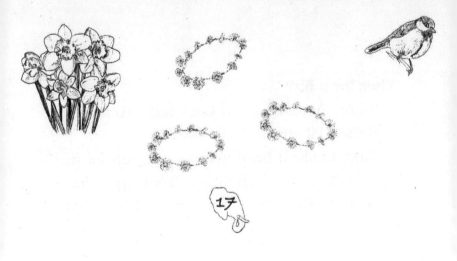

17

HESITATION

'Hi guys, I'd like you meet someone.'

Darryl's voice filled the yurt as he poked his head through the entrance the following Tuesday. Cleo and Tiegan were inside, but Ethan had decided to play football on the field. Spring had finally realised it was a time for daffodils and daisy chains as the warmer air drifted them towards the months of summer. As such, the teachers had finally allowed the children to play on the field again after a long winter, much to their delight.

A small boy, who looked to be about seven years old, hid shyly behind Darryl as he led him to the beanbags. Cleo recognised him as a boy she'd seen Emily teasing on the playground a few weeks ago. Emily, from her class, was a girl who she tried her best to avoid. She was mean to everyone except for her best friend, Lottie. There was even a rumour going round that Emily had caused Ben's injury at the talent show by swapping his block of wood for an extra hard one, knowing that he wouldn't be able to break it. Cleo didn't understand how anyone could do something so spiteful.

'This is Aaron. He's from Year 3,' said Darryl.

'Hi, Aaron,' Cleo and Tiegan said in unison, smiling at the boy.

He mumbled a small 'hi' back that was barely audible, quickly glancing away so that he didn't have to make eye contact with the two older girls.

'Aaron has been helping his dad look after his mum at home,' Darryl said, not elaborating any further. 'I told him about you guys and said I'd introduce you to each other in case he ever feels like popping into the yurt at break times.'

Cleo wondered whether Aaron's mum had an illness like her mum did but didn't want to pry. Aaron would tell them about it if and when he was ready to.

'Now, remember what I told you,' Darryl said, squatting down so that he was at the same height as Aaron. 'These girls are here every break time, so if you feel like you need any kind of support, you just come down and say hi, OK?'

'OK,' Aaron said, managing a tiny smile.

'How do you know we're in here every day?' asked Tiegan, looking suspiciously at Darryl.

'You girls have VIP access to *the* best place in Summercroft School,' he said, like it was obvious. 'Am I wrong?'

'No,' said Tiegan, laughing. 'We do come here a lot!'

As Darryl turned to take Aaron back out of the yurt, Cleo called after him, 'Welcome to The Elephant Squad, Aaron.'

'The Elephant Squad?' asked Darryl, raising his eyebrows inquisitively.

'Yep, it's the name of our club. Ethan thought of it. Do you like it?'

'Love it,' said Darryl. 'Named because elephants are such caring animals, right?'

'Yes!' exclaimed Cleo and Tiegan, as if they were one voice. 'How did you guess that so quickly?'

'What can I say?' said Darryl. 'I love nature shows. And you lot are true elephants!' With that, he ducked out of the yurt, taking Aaron with him.

'Do you think Aaron will come back another time?' Cleo asked Tiegan.

'Maybe. Do you think we should change the safe code to include his birthday numbers to make him feel welcome?'

'That's a good idea. Although, hang on a minute, you can only do eight numbers and we've already got eight. Besides, I've only just started to remember it without looking at the piece of paper we disguised it on. It would be silly to change it now. Let's make sure we look out for him on the playground though. I saw a girl from my class teasing him the other day, so I want to make sure I stick up for him if she does it again.'

'OK, let's make sure we pop out of the yurt every now and then at break times so we can check he's all right. That'll make him feel welcome. Someone else is bound to see one of our posters soon and realise that they can join us too. Aaron can't be the only one.'

'You'd think so, wouldn't you? They've been up for over a week now though and no-one else has come to see us.'

****

Unbeknown to Cleo and Tiegan, The Elephant Squad had nearly gained another new member earlier that day. A member that Ethan had been playing with on the Xbox the night before, without knowing his story. JammyJay, as he knew him, had played FIFA with Ethan until each of their mums had dragged them off at bedtime. Ethan usually had to get off the Xbox by 7.00pm, but his mum had had a meeting with the social worker about the new boy they had taken in last month, and time had run away with her. By the time she had cooked everyone dinner and got Sasha to bed, it was way past Ethan's usual cut-off time, and he had well and truly taken advantage. He figured that there must be some perks to sharing his mum with all these other kids!

The following day, as Jayden had psyched himself up to head over to the yurt, he had seen Darryl walking over there with a boy he recognised from Year 3. He'd once overheard his mum telling his dad how she felt sorry for this boy as this boy's mum could barely get out of bed some days as she was depressed. Jayden faltered as he questioned the idea of himself fitting into the mould of a young carer. This slight hesitation was all it took to make him doubt himself and change direction. Instead of heading over to become the newest member of The Elephant Squad, he ran towards the football pitch where he was swiftly passed the ball and joined his friends in their game.

HOPE

Jayden arrived at school on Friday morning feeling apprehensive but excited. His teacher had promised that she would let the class know after registration who had been selected for the creative writing session with the local author. Jayden hadn't mentioned it again to his mum since she had confirmed she'd received the email about it. He hadn't wanted to get his hopes up in case everyone else in the class also wanted to do it. If it came to pulling names out of a hat, he knew he wouldn't be one of the lucky ones. He'd always desperately wanted to win an Easter egg in the Easter raffle that the school held each year. Some children won every time, but no matter how many tickets he bought, his numbers were never the lucky ones. He knew that he would have exactly the same bad luck this time too.

The register seemed to drag on forever as everyone had to say *Good morning, Mrs Sullivan – Shepherd* when their name was called out. Jayden rolled his eyes as the fifth person responded with their ten-syllable greeting, which could have quite logically been replaced by a one-syllable *'yes'* or *'here'* to move things along quickly. Why his teacher, with her double-barrelled surname, thought it would be a good idea to do it this way, he would never know. Last year, he had a teacher who was so lazy that he didn't even say their names. His way of taking the register was for all the children to say their assigned number. At number twelve, all

148

Jayden had to do was listen out for his cue from number eleven, shout out his number twelve as the cue for number thirteen, and job done. None of this 'Good morning, Mrs Sullivan-Shepherd' malarkey. Last year's teacher would have signed ten people off the register before Mrs Sullivan-Shepherd had even ticked her first person off.

After an excruciating ten minutes of hearing the same reply thirty times, Jayden leant forward on the table in anticipation. You could almost hear a pin drop as everyone waited to hear what she would to say.

'Well, children, I am very proud to tell you that fifteen of you have shown an interest in the creative writing session which fills my heart with happiness that so many of you realise what a great opportunity this is for you.'

Jayden felt his heart sink as he knew that this meant that five of them would be disappointed.

'As you remember, I said that only ten of you would be able to go, so unfortunately that means five of you won't be able to join them. But I'll make it up to you by running my own little fun writing session here in class.'

Great, thought Jayden sarcastically. *Ten kids get to go to an exciting session run by a real-life, famous author, whilst the rest get stuck in the classroom having their creativity squashed by having grammar drummed into them.*

'Now, I printed off all your permission emails from your parents earlier, so I'll just pop them in this hat here...'

'Isn't all that printing bad for the environment?' a girl called Luna shouted out whilst Mrs Sullivan-Shepherd was rummaging behind her desk for the hat.

'Well, yes, I guess I didn't really need to print them,' admitted the teacher, looking a bit embarrassed to be told off by a child.

'You could have just written their names

on tiny bits of paper instead,' Luna suggested helpfully. 'Then you wouldn't have killed so many trees.'

'Yes, well it's a bit late now, Luna,' she said, looking a little irritated. 'But I will bear it in mind for future, thank you.'

Satisfied that she had done her bit for the Eco-Warrior team at school and educated her own teacher, Luna sat back in her seat looking smug, whilst Jayden tried to prepare himself for the inevitable let-down of not being one of the lucky ten.

'OK, here we go,' said the teacher as she rummaged her hand around in the large straw hat that looked like she had borrowed it from a scarecrow.

Although Jayden felt certain he wouldn't hear his name, there was still a glimmer of hope that he couldn't ignore as he listened intently...

'Alicia... Bruno... Thomas... Katie... Millie... Joseph...'

Jayden felt his shoulders sink a little

more with every name he heard that wasn't his.

'Max... William... Annabel... and last, but not least, Ja...'

Jaydon held his breath as he heard his teacher say the start of his name.

'...mie,' she finished.

Releasing the breath, it puffed out loudly through his lips. *Jamie... the teacher had said Jamie, not Jayden.* He felt struck with disappointment.

The children whose names had been called out murmured excitedly to each other, looking forward to the event which would take place the following Monday.

'I'm really sorry to the five of you whose names didn't get chosen,' said the teacher. 'Reuben, Georgia, Tamara, Joshua, and Hannah – if there is another opportunity next term, you five will be the first on the list, I promise.'

Jayden sat despondent at his desk. He rested his chin on his hands, feeling miserable. He'd really loved the idea of meeting the famous author and getting some advice about his writing. He'd wanted to ask what he needed to do to publish his own book one day. Now he'd never get the chance. *Hang on a minute,* he thought. *Why didn't the teacher say my name just now?*

Jayden put his hand up. 'You didn't say my name.'

'Why would I have said your name, Jayden?' Mrs Sullivan-Shepherd replied with an edge of exasperation to her voice. 'I told you I was reading out the names of the children who would be going to the creative writing session. Come on, wake up, pay attention.'

'I know,' replied Jayden, feeling both confused and irritated by his teacher's condescending tone. 'But my name wasn't pulled out of the hat, and you didn't say it just now when saying sorry to the others. You said Reuben, Georgia, Tamara, Joshua, and Hannah, but you didn't say, me.'

'That's because your name wasn't in the hat, Jayden,' said the teacher. 'Your mum didn't reply to the email to let us know you were interested.'

Before Jayden could say another word, the teacher turned her attention to the screen and flicked on her first slide about the Antarctic.

Jayden felt his cheeks tinge red as the penny dropped as to why his name hadn't been in the straw hat. His mum must have forgotten to reply to the email. She'd told Jayden that she'd received it so he had assumed that meant she'd also replied to it, but she must have forgotten. *No doubt, she'd been distracted by Seb,* he thought. Jayden felt his breathing quicken and realised his fingertips were stinging where he was digging his thumb nails into them. He'd felt disappointed when his name hadn't been selected, but this was different. He felt angry now, really angry. This had been important to him, and his mum had let him down.

Jayden felt his body tense up, and his head started to hurt – a deep throbbing in his temples that made his eyes feel strained. Everything around him became a blur as he stood up, screeching his chair against the floor as he did so. He couldn't bear to be in the classroom for a second longer. He needed to get out. Glaring at his teacher, who had turned around at the sound of the chair moving, Jayden stormed out of the door without a backward glance.

19

THE STRAW THAT BROKE THE CAMEL'S BACK

Cleo and Tiegan sat on their beanbags comparing notes. They had adopted their designated seats like families do on sofas at home. Tiegan wouldn't ever dream of sitting on the yellow beanbag – that was Cleo's. Cleo had pondered the thought of hiding it away so that no other child could ever sit on it when visiting the yurt for their reading sessions. She had quickly decided that would be far too selfish though – and there was also the issue that the open space within the yurt meant there was little opportunity to hide things.

'So, who have you come up with on your list?' asked Tiegan.

Despite their inviting posters being displayed across the school, Cleo, Tiegan, and Ethan were yet to welcome any other children into their support group other than the boy from Year 3 who had popped in to say hello with Darryl the other day. The girls had decided that it was time for them to do some detective work.

'Well, the new boy in my class, Ben Collins, is late to school a lot,' replied Cleo. 'But he never seems to miss out on things.'

'Hmm,' pondered Tiegan, looking thoughtful. 'Not your usual suspect, but let's keep him in mind just in case. His brother did sneak those biscuits from Darryl, so it could be that their mum and dad can't make them breakfast.'

'Very true,' Cleo agreed, trying to copy Tiegan's serious face. Inwardly she was thinking to herself that she was sure Ben Collins' younger brother was just incredibly cheeky and topping up on the delicious pancakes she'd overheard Ben telling Tommy that his mum makes. She probably shouldn't have even told Tiegan that he was a possibility for their group, but she didn't have an awful lot else to report and didn't want to let Tiegan down by saying nothing.

'How about you?'

'Well,' said Tiegan, looking thoughtful. 'There is this one girl in my class who is always getting told off for not doing her homework.'

'Maybe she just doesn't like doing homework,' suggested Cleo.

'Maybe. But maybe she just doesn't have time to do it because she's helping her parents with something.'

'Let's keep her in mind,' replied Cleo, copying what Tiegan had said to her about Ben. She had been excited at the thought of playing detective to decipher whether any other kids at school needed their help, but it hadn't turned out to be as much fun as she'd thought. Before the girls could compare notes any further, Ethan ran into the yurt.

'Have you guys heard what happened?' he asked, breathless from running.

'No,' they replied in unison.

'A boy called Jayden in Year 4 ran out of class today and the teachers can't find him.'

'Why did he run out?' asked Cleo.

'Apparently, he didn't get chosen for the workshop with that famous author,' Ethan said shrugging.

'Wow, he must have been really disappointed to react like that,' said Tiegan. She would be far too scared of getting in trouble to leave the class without the teacher's permission.

'Maybe there's more to it,' suggested Cleo, still in detective mode. 'Maybe he has stuff going on at home, and this is that one thing that sent him over the edge.'

'Like the straw that broke the camel's back,' said Tiegan, wanting to show off her knowledge of the phrase she'd heard her mum use.

'What if we were the ones to find him?' Cleo said, feeling excited at the prospect. 'Darryl said that we're stronger than we know because of how resilient our roles at home have made us. If we put our heads together and come up with all the places we would go if we felt at the end of our tether, we might find him.'

'I know what we need to do guys,' interrupted Tiegan, wanting to be the one to take charge. 'We need to put ourselves in his shoes and think where we would go.'

'That's exactly what Cleo just said,' said Ethan, looking quizzically at Tiegan.

Giving him the older girl look of superiority, Tiegan chose to ignore his observation and didn't reply.

'The toilets,' suggested Cleo, happy to let Tiegan take credit for her idea. She didn't feel the need to be the leader as Tiegan obviously did.

'Behind the curtain in front of the stage in the hall?' said Ethan.

'Those places are far too obvious,' said Tiegan with a tone of authority. 'Surely the teachers already looked there. We need to think outside the box.'

'What if he climbed over the gate and went out of school?' said Ethan with wide eyes.

'No-one would do that!' exclaimed Tiegan. 'They'd get in so much trouble. They may even get themselves expelled.'

The three children looked at each other with worried eyes. No-one had ever been expelled from Summercroft School before. Surely, they wouldn't expel Jayden... would they?

'We need to find him before that can happen,' said Cleo. She felt a strange sense of the need to protect this boy whom she hadn't even spoken to before. Her instincts told her that there was more to this than met the eye; not just the disappointed of not to being chosen for something.

'But how are we meant to find him if he's not in school?' asked Ethan. 'I don't know about you guys, but I'm not planning on jumping over the gate any time soon.'

'Well, that is the worst-case scenario,' said Tiegan. 'Let's assume we're not at that point yet and worry about it when we've exhausted all other possibilities.'

One by one, the children brainstormed ideas of where someone might hide successfully in a school full of children and teachers. Stationary cupboards... the PE shed... under the teacher's desk... between the bookshelves in the library. When they put their minds to it, there were actually more potential hiding places than they had first realised.

'I'd hide here in the yurt if it was me,' said Cleo.

'Me too,' agreed Tiegan. 'Although it's probably the first place they'd look for us.'

'Why've you stacked the beanbags up in the corner like that?' asked Ethan, wriggling his feet which were going numb from being tucked underneath him as he sat on his beanbag. He'd been so desperate to share in the drama about the missing boy that he hadn't noticed that he had plonked himself down on the bright lime green beanbag rather than his usual maroon coloured one. Four of the beanbags, including *his* one, were missing from their usual semi-circle formation.

'We didn't,' said Tiegan, looking at the corner that Ethan was pointing to. 'That's not a corner anyway,' she said in a know-it-all voice. 'The yurt is round, so how can it have any corners?'

'Maybe the last reading group left them like that for some reason,' Cleo said absent-mindedly, as she stood up. She was used to keeping her house tidy to prevent her mum from tripping over things, and her instincts made her automatically get up to put the beanbags back where they belonged.

She grabbed the loop on the maroon bag which had been stacked at the top of the pile – which was probably what had caused Ethan to notice it. The beanbag should have lifted easily given that the polystyrene balls within it were as light as a feather. Cleo remembered when her beanbag at home had burst when she was a toddler. She had fond memories of the balls scattering over her bedroom floor, creating the perfect surface for snow angels. Her mum hadn't been quite as thrilled by the sight as Cleo had been – she had still been vacuuming up the tiny little white balls weeks later.

But the beanbag at the top of the pile *didn't* lift easily. Something was putting resistance against it, making it impossible for Cleo to pull it up. She tried pulling the one underneath it which always reminded her of a ladybird with its bright red material and big splats of black. She managed to pull it slightly, but it slipped out of her hand as something tugged it back down.

'Hey, guys,' Cleo said, glancing back at Tiegan and Ethan. 'Can you come over here a sec?'

Heaving themselves up from their beanbags, the other two wandered over to see what Cleo wanted.

Cleo put her finger to her lips to indicate they should shush, and then, widening her eyes, she nodded her head towards the stack of beanbags.

Tiegan squinted her eyes, wondering what Cleo was getting at, but Ethan seemed to be on the same wavelength as her and widened his own eyes, making an O-shape with his mouth. Cleo indicated for her friends to grab hold of the maroon beanbag with her and then mouthed *one, two, three.* On three, they all tugged together. Unable this time to resist their combined force, the beanbag flew up in their hands to reveal a head. Tiegan, still not quite realising the direction events were going, screamed at the unexpected sight. You could forgive her for being a little alarmed, as the way the other beanbags were positioned did make it look as though a lone, bodyless head was resting on them.

The boy, whose eyes met theirs, looked flushed where his body heat had been trapped in by the beanbags he'd been huddled under for so long. His red-rimmed eyes looked sad as he gazed at the group of children whom he had thought about coming to join before but had never quite made it. He hadn't intended to seek them out today, but when he had run out of the classroom, this was where his legs had brought him – as if on instinct. He had felt that this would be a safe place for him to go to let out his emotions – all the frustration and anger that he couldn't contain today, no matter how hard he had tried or how many deep breaths he had taken.

'Hi,' said Cleo. 'I'm guessing you must be Jayden.'

REALISATION

Jayden looked up at the three pairs of eyes that were staring at him. He had been getting a bit claustrophobic squashed behind all the beanbags so wasn't wholly disappointed that his hiding place had finally been discovered. Also because it was other kids who had discovered him and not the teachers.

'Everyone's been looking for you,' Ethan said when Jayden didn't answer.

Jayden just shrugged his shoulders like he had no interest in hearing this.

Tiegan cleared her throat, regaining her composure after her embarrassing scream when the 'bodyless head' appeared.

'Why did you run out of your classroom like that?'

She still couldn't believe how anyone would be that bold. Jayden just glared at her rather than answering.

'Is it because you didn't get picked to meet that author?' she persisted.

Jayden gave a sneery chuckle and shook his head. He knew that's what it would look like to everyone. But it wasn't as simple as that. His emotions had made him run out of the classroom. Emotions that had been building up in him for a very long time. Emotions that he'd kept hidden from his mum and dad because they already had so much to cope with because of his brother. Emotions that he'd kept hidden from his friends because they just wouldn't understand. Emotions that Jayden didn't even understand himself sometimes.

Having a younger brother with autism could be difficult. Jayden loved Seb and knew that he needed his support as he didn't always see the world in the same way as others. Seb felt overwhelmed by things a lot of the time and struggled to make friends. This made Jayden feel guilty for having lots of friends. It made him feel responsible for being the one to make his brother happy. It made him feel like he had to put his brother's needs before his own, just like his parents always seemed to. And thinking this made Jayden feel guilty all over again, as he knew that it wasn't his parent's fault – Seb just needed them more.

Jayden had all this going around in his head whilst most eight- and nine-year-olds just worried about whether the school roast dinner would be the delicious chicken or the stringy gammon that took all of lunch time to chew. This wasn't about missing out on something he'd wanted to do. This was an accumulation of all the missed days out because Seb couldn't cope with the busy crowds, the missed homework because Seb needed his help, the missed sleep because Seb kept him awake, and now the missed opportunity to meet the author because Seb had distracted his mum when she had said she'd respond to the email. Jayden had more inner strength than a lot of children his age, but today he was the camel and when that last straw was placed on him, he came crashing down.

'No, it's not about not getting picked,' he finally replied to Tiegan when the three children continued to stare at him. 'Well, yeah, I guess it kind of is, but no, not just that.'

'What else then?' asked Tiegan.

She knew she was being nosy, but as self-appointed leader of The Elephant Squad, she felt that it was her duty.

'Just stuff,' Jayden said, pushing the rest of the beanbags off himself. The other children stepped back as he stood up. He was nearly as tall as Ethan, despite being in the year below.

'Do you want to tell us about it?' Cleo asked in a less direct way. She couldn't shake the feeling that this boy had come to the yurt for a reason. He could have chosen any of the other hiding places that they had come up with, but he had picked the yurt. Whether it was a conscious decision or not, his instincts had led him here.

Jayden shrugged his shoulders again, but his eyes didn't look angry anymore. The yurt was filled with silence, and the children were suddenly aware that the hum of noise from the playground had stopped.

'Why's it gone so quiet outside?' Ethan asked, walking over to the yurt entrance.

'Erm, guys,' he said turning around, looking worried. 'I think break time may have finished already.'

'But we'd have heard the bell,' said Tiegan. 'We always hear the bell.'

'Maybe it went at the same time as you

screamed,' said Cleo.

Tiegan looked embarrassed. 'I didn't scream that loud.'

'You did scream pretty loud,' said Ethan, laughing. 'It reminded me of a fox that was screeching outside my window one night.'

A small smile etched itself across Jayden's lips as he witnessed the banter between these three friends.

'But we're going to get into so much trouble,' said Tiegan, looking worried. The only times that she had been late for school were last year when her gran had first come to live with them, but now that she was in Year 6, she walked herself to school. She loved the independence of not having to rely on anyone else. The responsibility of arriving at school on time was all hers and she was never late. Now, she was going to be back late from break time. She hated the thought of getting told off.

'No, we won't,' said Cleo, confidently. 'Not when we tell the teachers that we found

Jayden.'

Cleo smiled at Jayden questioningly. 'You are Jayden, aren't you?' She was ninety-nine percent certain but realised that Jayden hadn't actually confirmed either way when she had made the assumption upon finding him under the beanbags.

'Yep,' he nodded. 'That's me.' And then, looking directly at Ethan, 'Otherwise known as JammyJay on the Xbox.'

Ethan smiled as the penny dropped about who he'd been playing with. He'd known it was a boy in Year 4, but he hadn't been able to put a face to the name.

'You've got some skills in *FIFA*,' Ethan complimented Jayden.

Jayden smiled, feeling embarrassed by the praise. Turning his attention to the group, he confirmed what he already knew. 'And you're Cleo, right? And you're Tiegan, and you're Ethan,' he said, looking at each of them in turn. They may have been in different year groups, but Jayden had taken note of the children going into the yurt on the lunch times when he had pondered going to join them. He knew exactly who these children were.

'Yep, we're The Elephant Squad,' Cleo said proudly.

'The Elephant Squad?' questioned Jayden, raising his eyebrows.

'Yep,' confirmed Tiegan, taking charge of the explanation. 'Because an elephant is one of the most caring animals on the planet. And we all care for someone at home.'

Jayden was quiet for a moment and then, feeling a connection with the other three children in the yurt, he finally voiced what he had been thinking for a while now.

'I think that maybe I do too.'

KIND HEART

'Hey guys,' announced Darryl as he joined the children in the yurt the following Friday. It had been a week since Jayden had officially met The Elephant Squad, and a school day hadn't passed since without them meeting up. After sharing the story of his home life with the others, Jayden felt like a weight had been lifted from him as they all understood and empathised.

The children looked up as Darryl walked in through the entrance. They were always pleased to see him. And not just because he had great taste in biscuits, which he had recently started bringing along with him again whenever he visited. They all had Ethan to thank for that after he'd mentioned to Darryl that there were never any biscuits left in his biscuit tin at home thanks to Sasha's love of custard creams!

'Hi, Jayden, nice to see you again.'

When the children hadn't returned to their classes after break time on the day that Jayden went missing, a teacher had come to the yurt looking for them. As Cleo had predicted, any punishment that might have planned was soon forgotten when the teacher saw that they had found Jayden. The head teacher had been moments away from contacting the police, as his worst-case-scenario train of thought led him to think that Jayden must have jumped over the school gates. Finding him safe and sound in the yurt had made The Elephant Squad the heroes of the day, rather than truants in need of punishment. And with the help of their explanation as to why Jayden had run out of the classroom, the teachers had decided that Jayden could escape any consequences too. Instead, they gave Darryl a call, who dropped everything he was doing and came to the school to talk things through with Jayden.

'Hi, Darryl,' Jayden said, now smiling.

'I have something I wanted to talk to you about,' said Darryl. 'Something, I think you're going to like the sound of.'

All eyes homed in on Darryl as he directed his attention to the newest member of their squad. Usually, Darryl just asked them how things were at home and got them talking about their feelings and any problems they were having, but this felt different. This felt like he was about to give Jayden some sort of good news.

Jayden looked at Darryl with intrigue,

having no clue as to what he might be about to say.

'I got in touch with Leo Sparks, the author that you missed out on meeting last week. I hope you don't mind, but I told him about your love of writing and how you have the ambition to write your own book one day.'

Jayden shuffled his feet, feeling a bit embarrassed. He'd surprised himself the other day by opening up to Darryl about his dream to be an author. He'd never told anyone else. He wasn't sure how he felt about the others now knowing too.

'So,' Darryl said, pausing for dramatic effect. 'How do you like the sound of a one-on-one session with Leo tomorrow afternoon?'

Jayden looked at Darryl, feeling utterly speechless. His mouth slowly got wider and wider as he brought his left hand up to cover it. Finally, he found his voice.

'Just me?' he asked.

'Yes, just you,' Darryl confirmed, smiling.

'And he said to tell you that if you have an idea for a story, bring it along, and he'll give you some pointers.'

Jayden couldn't believe what he was hearing. He had had an idea for a story just last night, and he'd jotted it down in his notepad. And now he was going to be able to share his idea with an actual real-life author who could give him advice. This was way better than attending a workshop with fifty other kids. A smile began to break out across Jayden's face. A smile so big it would be contagious to even the grumpiest of souls.

****

Moments after Darryl had left the children in the yurt, he turned around at the sound of Cleo calling to him as she ran to catch him up.

'Hey, Cleo, everything OK?'

'I just had a thought,' said Cleo, a little

breathless after her short run after him.

'What if we could do something really nice for Ethan and Tiegan too?' she said, widening her eyes with enthusiasm. 'Jayden is so happy that you've arranged the one-to-one with the author for him, and it made me think, what if we could make the others that happy too.'

Darryl smiled at Cleo as she blurted all this out without taking a breath. When he didn't answer immediately, Cleo raised her eyebrows and prompted him, 'What do you think?'

'I think, Cleo, that you have one of the kindest hearts I have ever known.'

'So, is that a yes then?'

'Yes, it's a huge yes,' said Darryl. 'I think it's a wonderful idea.'

Cleo beamed at him, feeling chuffed that he liked her suggestion and even more chuffed at his compliment that she had a kind heart.

'So, what do you want to do for them

then?' asked Darryl.

'Well, I keep thinking how Ethan sometimes has to miss out on doing stuff with his mum as she has to drop everything to help the new foster kids,' said Cleo. 'Do you remember how, when we first met him, he said that he was meant to go to the cinema on the Saturday but they had to cancel it at the last minute as the social worker asked his mum to take that boy in?'

'Yeah, I remember. He was so accepting of it, wasn't he?'

'Yeah, which makes me think it happens quite a lot,' said Cleo. 'So, I was thinking that maybe one night we could set up the yurt as a cinema and watch the movie he missed here with him. It's bound to be available to download by now. I could go home after school to see my mum and then come back. And I'll have the phone here so I can call her and check on her...'

Darryl rubbed his chin as if pondering the possibility. When Cleo didn't get a response straight away, her excited face was quickly replaced by a frown. 'Do you think it's a stupid idea?'

'No, no,' Darryl reassured her. 'I think it's a great idea. I'm just contemplating how to convince your head teacher to let me bring the big screen from the hall down here. You leave that to me though,' he said with a wink. 'I'll sort out all the finer details. You just need to keep it a secret from Ethan so it's a nice surprise for him.'

Cleo's grin returned to her face as he said this. She had no doubt that Darryl would do whatever he had to do to convince their grouchy head teacher to let them go ahead. Darryl was one of those proactive, positive people who could make this happen. Cleo was sure of it!

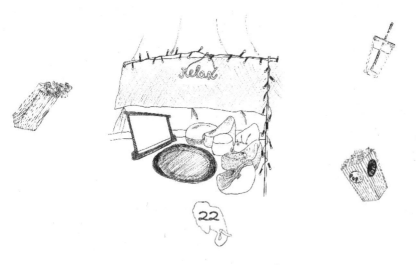

THE SURPRISE

Cleo's faith in Darryl was justified as he used his powers of persuasion to convince Mr Growler to allow him to remove the big screen from the hall and temporarily set it up in the yurt.

Cleo gazed around her in delight as she took in the transformation that she and Darryl had been working on since 6.00pm that evening. She couldn't believe how quickly they had made it happen after her initial idea just five days earlier. When Cleo had asked her mum if it would be OK, she was completely supportive of the idea. She had felt fine knowing that Cleo would come home from school to check on her and help her with dinner and then return to school for just a few hours.

With the warmer weather that had set in recently, the days were now getting longer as the sun set later in the evening. The downside of this meant that the light-coloured material of the yurt made it far too bright for their makeshift cinema. Darryl had had the great idea to pin up black material on the yurt walls, which Cleo had then draped fairy lights over. She had also brought the neon *Relax* sign from her room that glowed a fluorescent yellow in the now darkened interior. Their favourite beanbags, plus the daisy chain one that Darryl seemed to favour, were lined up in a row in front of the big screen. Connected to the screen was Darryl's own laptop that he had brought in from his house to stream the movie through.

Cleo had lined up huge cups filled to the brim with lemonade. Each cup had a paper straw in it which had been personalised with glittery blue writing which read 'Ethan's Big Movie Night'. The cups sat on the trestle table upon which Darryl had plated up his biscuits when they had first met in the yurt those few months ago. Next to each cup sat a tub of toffee popcorn which Cleo had subtly found out was Ethan's favourite. There were also five cartons of pick 'n' mix sweets laid out – Cleo had insisted to Darryl that he share in all the movie snacks, and he didn't protest!

As the yurt had no power, Darryl had expertly laid out the world's longest extension lead all the way to the nearest classroom. When it didn't quite reach through the door, he cleverly pushed it through an open window, reaching the plug socket with just centimetres to spare. Cleo had crossed her fingers and even her toes as she had watched through the entrance of the yurt, knowing that if Darryl didn't succeed, the whole movie night would be over.

'I think we're ready,' Darryl said turning round to grin at Cleo as he used the remote controller to pause the movie on the title screen. 'Now we just need to wait for Tiegan, Jayden, and Ethan to arrive for their very important 'Elephant Squad meeting."

Cleo giggled. She had told her three friends that Darryl had asked them all to meet here in the yurt to discuss a new child he had suspected of needing their help. After suspiciously questioning why this meeting needed to be in the evening after school, Cleo had had to let Jayden and Tiegan in on the secret plan. With their help, Ethan had finally accepted the story and agreed to return to school when Cleo had told him that Darryl had promised that he'd bring biscuits.

Poking her head out of the yurt again, she saw the rest of The Elephant Squad walking together up the field.

'They're coming!' she squealed excitedly to Darryl.

Tiegan, unsurprisingly, adopted the role of leader, walking a few paces ahead and guiding the rest of the troop inside. She gasped at the sight of the transformation of the yurt and turned around to see Ethan's reaction as he walked in with Jayden.

'What the...?'

Ethan stopped in shock as he took in his surroundings that were so familiar yet so different from the last time he had set foot in them.

'Surprise!' shouted Cleo, Tiegan, Jayden, and Darryl, all at once, like they had planned.

'What the...?' Ethan repeated as his mouth dropped open an inch. He moved his eyes around the room, taking in the delights of the drinks and munchies on the table. The fairy lights twinkled around the yurt as he noticed the row of beanbags, and then he saw it – the screen so large it was impossible to miss, emblazoned with the image of the movie he had wanted to see all those months ago. The trip out with his mum that had had to be dropped like a hot potato when another child needed their help.

'We thought you deserved your very own, personal cinema,' Darryl said stepping forward to Ethan. 'Or rather, Cleo had the great idea, and I just helped a little to make it happen.'

'This is amazing,' Ethan said, shaking his head in wonder.

Cleo thought that he looked like he had a bit of a tear in his eye as he acknowledged what his friends had done for him. Before he could get all emotional, she grabbed a tub of the toffee popcorn and thrust it at him.

'Your favourite, I believe!'

Ethan laughed, taking it from her. 'So that's why you asked me to play that game of *Would You Rather*,' he said, realising that there had been more to it than a harmless game to relieve their boredom the other day. He remembered Cleo slipping in the *'Would you rather eat toffee popcorn or sweet and salty popcorn?'* between *'Would you rather eat worms or maggots?'* and *'Would you rather be changed into a baby for the day or a ninety-year-old man?'*

Without delay they all grabbed their snacks and drinks and jumped onto their favourite beanbags as the title music filled the yurt.

'I can't believe you set up surround sound too!' Ethan exclaimed, seeing the speakers either side of the screen. 'This is better than a real cinema!'

Cleo felt a glow of warm happiness spread through her as she saw how happy Ethan was. Now she just needed to run her idea for Tiegan past Darryl. *That can wait for now though,* she thought to herself as she let her body sink into her beanbag and popped a tangy sweet from her pick n' mix bag into her mouth, fixing her eyes on the big screen in front of her. She had a whole hour to relax and enjoy the movie before Darryl stopped it for an interval to let her quickly call her mum to check she was OK.

GETTING YOUR HOPES
UP

After the success of the movie night, Cleo couldn't wait to talk to Darryl about her plan for Tiegan. First though, she wanted to find out a bit more from her mum – as she, after all, was the one who had given Cleo the idea.

'Hi, Mum, I'm home. Are you OK?'

'Hi, sweetheart. Yes, absolutely fine. Did you have fun?' her mum called from the kitchen.

'It was so good! I'm bursting for a wee though. I don't know how I made it home without wetting myself after drinking that huge cup of lemonade.'

As Cleo ran to the toilet, she thought she heard another voice in the kitchen. Furrowing her eyebrows, she wondered who it might be. Finishing on the toilet as quickly as she could, Cleo washed her hands and dashed the short distance to the kitchen. She was startled to see Ben Collins from school sitting at her kitchen table with a lady whom she recognised from the talent show. Sitting on the floor next to Ben was the most adorable golden cocker spaniel dog that Cleo had ever set eyes on. Letting out a high pitched 'Awwww' noise, she rushed over and started stroking the dog's floppy ears.

Cleo was just about to ask Ben what the dog's name was, when she remembered shouting to her mum about nearly wetting herself. Feeling mortified that Ben would have undoubtedly heard her, she fixed her eyes on his dog, glad to have an excuse not to make eye contact with anyone.

'This is Ben's mum, Amber,' Cleo's mum said, introducing her. 'They were in the next road along taking Obi for a walk when I called them, so they said they'd pop in. Isn't that a co-incidence!'

Aw, so his name's Obi, thought Cleo. *Cute name!*

'It is a bit,' agreed Cleo, forcing herself to look at Amber to be polite. She felt puzzled as to why her mum would be calling Ben's mum but felt a bit rude asking. Her mum could always read her like a book though and elaborated without her daughter having to ask.

'Amber is the lady I was telling you about,' she said. 'The one who's a ghostwriter for people's autobiographies.'

'Oh!' said Cleo as the penny dropped. When her mum had told her about one of the mums from school who wrote books about people's lives, she had no idea that it was Ben's mum she'd been talking about. They'd been having their usual chat over dinner one evening, where they told each other one good thing about their day and one bad thing. Getting the bad things out the way first, Cleo's mum had told her about finding a hole in her favourite jumper, and Cleo had told her mum about walking into assembly with a piece of toilet paper stuck to the bottom of her shoe. She would have discreetly removed it had it not been for that spiteful Emily pointing it out and sniggering to the rest of the class. After reassuring her daughter that the toilet paper incident would happen to everyone at least once in their lifetime, Cleo's mum had told her about Amber. When she had said that Amber was a ghostwriter, Cleo had initially thought that she must write scary stories about ghosts. Quickly realising that she was about to give her daughter nightmares, Cleo's mum had explained that a ghostwriter was a writer who let someone else take the credit for the writing – in this case, the person that Amber was writing about. Cleo had loved hearing how she had written a book for a lady with Alzheimer's so that her family could have her memories captured before they faded. She had instantly thought of Tiegan and her gran. Knowing that Tiegan would love to have her own memory book so she could always remember her gran as she was, Cleo had asked her mum if they could talk to Amber about writing her one. Not knowing how expensive it would be, Cleo had asked her mum to call Amber and find out.

Looking at Amber now, Cleo noticed how her eyes were identical to Ben's. She remembered thinking on his first day in school how blue they were, and his mum's were that same blue but with more wrinkles on the skin around them.

'Your mum told me about you wanting to do something special for your friend,' Amber said to Cleo, smiling. 'I think that's such a lovely idea.'

Cleo smiled back shyly. She had never been very good at accepting compliments without getting embarrassed. She busied herself tickling Obi's ears again.

'He likes his tummy being tickled too,' said Ben, reaching round to Obi's soft belly. Obi instantly flopped to the floor and rolled onto his back. Following Ben's lead, Cleo moved her hand to Obi's belly as his tail wagged so hard that she could feel a breeze on her arm.

Cleo looked at her mum, desperate to know if she had found out whether they could afford the book for Tiegan. Again, her mum read her mind with the wonder of their mother-daughter telepathy.

'The books do cost quite a bit, love.'

And then looking at Amber she quickly added, 'and rightly so with the amount of work that Amber puts into them.'

'But,' interrupted Amber. 'I have told your

mum that I will do an extra special discount for you.'

Cleo smiled, feeling excited that she might actually be able to pull this off. She knew that Darryl had a small amount of money that he was allowed to spend on things for the groups that he set up. Now, she just needed to find out if his budget would stretch to doing this for Tiegan. The movie night for Ethan had cost no more than the price of the movie and snacks. However, this was a different thing entirely, and although Cleo was optimistic, she didn't want to get her hopes up in case they came crashing down.

TOFFEE POPCORN AND

TRUST

Cleo glanced out of the opening of the yurt to make sure Tiegan wasn't about to bound in and overhear her conversation.

When the teacher had announced break time, Cleo had shot out of the door faster than a dog who'd caught whiff of a sausage. She had been thinking about the phone call she needed to make to Darryl all morning and was determined to get to the yurt before

Tiegan disturbed her. After getting the safe code wrong twice in her haste, the phrase *third time lucky* rang true as the door unlocked and she reached in to grab The Elephant Squad phone. Finding Darryl's name on the short list of contacts, she'd hit call and breathed a sigh of relief when he answered on the first ring.

Cleo wasn't disappointed with Darryl's response. After her brief but enthusiastic explanation of her plan to surprise Tiegan, he had readily agreed. The only problem was that the cost of the surprise was far greater than Darryl's funds would allow.

However, he was quick to reassure Cleo when she sounded deflated upon hearing this.

'You could do something that people will sponsor you for. Maybe get Ethan and Jayden involved too. Just set up a page on a sponsorship website explaining why you're doing it and ask people to share it to spread the word.'

Cleo couldn't stop herself grinning as she heard this suggestion and forgot for a minute that she was meant to be on the lookout for Tiegan. She jumped as her friend suddenly appeared in the yurt.

'Tiegan!' she gasped.

'Hi, Cleo,' Tiegan replied, taken aback by her loud greeting. 'Everything OK?'

'Yes, fine,' Cleo said looking guilty. And then into the phone she said, 'OK, Mum, glad you're OK. See you in a couple of hours.'

Realising that they had been rumbled, Darryl played along, allowing Cleo to quickly hang up.

'How good was that movie night!' exclaimed Tiegan as she flopped down onto her beanbag. She looked around the yurt and shook her head. 'It looks so normal again in here now. It's hard to imagine it all blacked out like a cinema. 'What was your favourite bit, Cleo.'

'Definitely the toffee popcorn,' said Cleo.

'No, silly,' laughed Tiegan. 'I meant what was your favourite bit of the movie!'

Before Cleo could give her answer, Jayden and Ethan bounded in. The girls smiled at them, pleased that Jayden saw the yurt as his base now too.

'What was your favourite bit the other night?' persisted Tiegan, looking at the boys.

'The toffee popcorn,' they both answered in unison.

As Tiegan dramatically put her head in her hands, making Cleo laugh, the boys looked at each other, shrugging their shoulders, completely baffled as to what they had said wrong.

'Forget it,' said Tiegan, getting up to leave the yurt. 'I only popped in for a minute. I need to go to the office because I forgot to bring my PE kit today, so I need to borrow one.' Pausing, she turned around and looked at her friends. 'Actually, that's a lie. I didn't forget my PE kit. My gran tried to do the washing yesterday and mistook some pink paint for the washing liquid. So now my PE kit is a mottled pink colour.'

The other children looked at her for a minute, wondering how to respond as Tiegan's face changed from sadness to laughter. They started laughing with her as they all chose to find the humour in her situation.

'It was my own fault,' said Tiegan. 'I left the paint next to the washing machine the other day. Anyone could have mistaken it for washing liquid, right?'

'Right,' they all agreed as the laughter subsided.

'I've got a spare PE kit that someone gave my mum years ago when they left the school,' said Cleo. 'It's too big for me. I'll bring it into school tomorrow for you.'

Tiegan smiled at Cleo, feeling thankful that she had some friends that she could be herself with and tell them the truth about how hard things sometimes were at home.

'Now,' said Cleo conspiratorially as Tiegan exited the yurt. 'I have something that I need your help with.'

Ethan and Jayden looked at her, intrigued by the tone in her voice.

'I've had a great idea about something nice we can do for Tiegan, and I need you guys to help me.'

As Cleo filled the others in on her plan for Tiegan, they put their heads together to come up with an idea for sponsorship. Between the three of them, they came up with lots of suggestions, such as a readathon, a cake sale, a fun run, and a car wash, but by far the best idea they had was Ethan's suggestion to get a teacher to sit in a bath of cold baked beans. They decided that Jayden would use his amazing writing talent to write an evocative page to encourage people to donate money. Ethan offered to use his mum's laptop to set up the actual sponsorship page. So, all that was left for Cleo to do was to ask her mum to use her love of social media to share the page to spread the word. Oh, and to convince one of the teachers to be the one to sacrifice their ego for the good cause.

'But remember,' said Cleo as the bell rang to signal the end of break time. 'Not a word to Tiegan and nothing on the sponsorship page must give away who she is. She's very private about her gran so we mustn't break her trust on that one, OK?'

'OK,' the boys answered obediently. Like Cleo, they knew how important it was to be able to trust each other with the private things that they shared within The Elephant Squad.

THE BAKED BEAN

BATH

Thanks to Jayden's amazing talent with words, the public seemed to connect with the children's story about raising money for their friend to have a memento of her gran as her memory faded. Sadly, it would seem that Tiegan's story wasn't an unusual one and there were many other families out there losing a loved one to dementia. Within just two weeks, they had enough money to pay Ben's mum for the book, and they had managed to do it completely anonymously to protect Tiegan's privacy! True to her word, Ben's mum had given them a hefty discount, admiring the love and care they were showing to their friend.

Unfortunately, the teachers weren't so forthcoming with offering up their humiliation, and they had all opted to give a hefty donation rather than be the one to sit in a bath of cold baked beans.

Ethan had saved the day, however, and had promised to take one for the team. Hence, he was currently sitting in his bath at home, bracing himself for the inevitable. With the begrudging permission of his mum on the condition that he would thoroughly clean out the bath afterwards, he and Jayden had pulled open the lids of fifty baked bean cans ready to pour into the bath. Realising that it would actually take about four hundred cans to fill the bath, Jayden had cleverly suggested that they pad the bath out with towels before pouring the baked beans in to give the illusion that there were more in there than there actually were. They didn't feel like this was cheating as Ethan's body would still be covered in cold baked beans as he sat on top of the towels in his swimming shorts.

Jayden took great pleasure in picking up the first can and pouring it in from as high up as he could possibly reach. Ethan flinched as the cold sauce splatted on his legs, as Jayden's technique ensured maximum coverage as gravity propelled the baked beans downwards. He was surprised at how cold they were against his skin, and he shivered as sauce ran slowly between his toes. Laughing, Jayden grabbed the next can and wasted no time in pouring that one straight onto Ethan's stomach. Ethan squirmed as a baked bean lodged itself in his belly button.

'Ew, that feels horrible!' he exclaimed.

'Don't be a baby,' Jayden jeered good naturedly.

'I didn't see you volunteering to sit in this

bath!' challenged Ethan.

'Good point. I take it back. You are very brave and manly.'

'Just shut up and pour the baked beans,' laughed Ethan. 'Let's get this over with and get the photo for the sponsorship page so that people know that I did it.'

After the initial shock of the slimy, wet texture cascading over his bare skin, Ethan grabbed some cans himself and helped Jayden pour them into the bath. The distinct aroma of tomato sauce filled the room as the white tiled walls next to the bath became a mess of orange splashes.

Hearing Ethan and Jayden's laughter, Sasha ran into the bathroom to see what she was missing out on. Their newest foster brother, Adam, followed closely behind, and a smile broke out across his face as he couldn't quite believe what he was seeing.

'Grab a can!' Ethan said to him, realising that it was one of the few times he had seen him smile properly. 'It's not every day you'll get to pour bean sauce over me.'

Jayden handed him a can so he could join in the fun, and he only hesitated for a second before shaking a huge dollop out over Ethan's chest.

After five minutes of mayhem, Jayden allowed Sasha to pour the final can over Ethan's head and captured the moment on camera perfectly for their sponsorship page. Sasha squealed with delight at being given permission to do something so naughty as she watched the baked bean sauce dripping down Ethan's shocked face.

'Who wants a hug then?' Ethan asked, standing up in the bath and reaching out towards Sasha. Screaming, she fled the bathroom before she too could be covered in slimy goop. Jayden and Adam swiftly followed her.

'Oi, who's going to help me clean all this up?' shouted Ethan. When no-one responded, he decided there was only one person who could battle a mess of this enormity...

'Muuuuum, can you come and help me please!'

HAPPY TEARS

The Elephant Squad decided that the best way to tell Tiegan about her gift was to present her with a card, handmade by Cleo.

'What's this?' Tiegan asked in surprise as they all gathered around her in the yurt during Darryl's next visit. 'It's not my birthday.'

'We know that,' said Cleo, adopting the role of spokesperson. 'Just open it and see.'

Cleo rocked back and forth on her shoes, excited to see Tiegan's reaction when she realised what they had arranged for her.

An unusual silence filled the yurt as Tiegan ripped open the envelope containing the card. Cleo had spent an hour making it last night and felt proud of how it had turned out. She had found a picture of an elephant in an animal book that she had had since she was little. After her fourth attempt at trying to copy it, she had been satisfied with her efforts. The trunk was a little wonky, but her mum had told her that it gave the elephant character. She decorated the rest of the card with purple flowers, knowing that Tiegan choosing the purple beanbag wasn't just a coincidence. She loved the colour purple almost as much as Cleo loved yellow.

'Aw, that's such a cute card,' said Tiegan.

'Open it then!' said Cleo unable to contain her excitement.

As Tiegan opened the card, she read out loud the neat handwriting that Cleo had painstakingly perfected.

'Dear Tiegan. We wanted to do something nice for you so have arranged for a lady to write a book about your gran so that you can remember her how she was. We hope you like it. Lots of love, The Elephant Squad. Kiss, kiss, kiss, kiss.'

When Tiegan fell silent, Cleo felt her excitement waver as she suddenly wondered if she'd done the right thing.

'Don't you like it?' she asked gently.

When Tiegan looked up, she had tears in her eyes. She looked at her friends gathered around her, waiting to see her response. She wanted to say thank you, but she felt as though there was a lump in her throat, and for the first time in her life she was lost for words.

As Cleo bit her bottom lip, unsure what to say, Darryl took the lead.

'Are these happy tears or sad tears?' he asked tentatively.

Tiegan gave a little sniff and with her lip quivering she whispered, 'Both.'

Giving her a minute to compose herself, Darryl then prompted her to elaborate. He had always been amazing at getting the children to talk about their feelings, and all of them felt completely at ease with him, and each other.

'I'm sad because my gran is getting worse,' said Tiegan. 'Last night, she started playing Connect 4 with me and then stopped just as I was about to win saying that she didn't like losing to strangers.'

The others all looked at Tiegan with compassion, imagining how tough that must have been.

'And I'm happy because I met you guys and you're all so lovely. And I can't actually believe you have done this amazing thing for me.'

Cleo finally let out the breath that she didn't even realise she'd been holding, as she received the much-needed confirmation that her idea had been a good one.

THE FUNNY ONE...THE ANGRY ONE...THE CARING ONE...AND THE BOSSY ONE!

As the days grew even warmer, Summercroft School headed towards its final week before the much-anticipated summer holidays. The bond between the members of The Elephant Squad grew even stronger as they continued to meet in the yurt.

It was a rare day when it was just the four of them in there. Although initially slow to gain momentum, the eye-catching posters that they'd put up around the school had gradually encouraged other children to have the confidence to come forward. The Elephant Squad welcomed each child into the yurt with open arms, just as they had with Jayden.

Darryl had put a few games in there for them to play, but their favourite by far was Jenga. There was friendly competition between the original four Elephant Squad members as they pulled their blocks out, slowly and carefully. Of course, no-one ever wanted to be the one to topple the tower over. Tiegan was a stickler for the rules, being quick to reprimand if one of them sneakily tried to pick a new block after their initial choice refused to wiggle free.

'Have you finished writing your story yet?' Ethan asked Jayden as Jayden looked with immense concentration at the block he was manoeuvring.

'Stop trying to distract me,' he replied

good naturedly.

'I'm not trying to distract you,' Ethan laughed. 'Well, maybe a little.'

The blocks came crashing down as Jayden misjudged the pressure he had put on his chosen block.

'See, you distracted me,' he said, giving Ethan a look of mock anger.

'That block was never going to come out cleanly, Jayden,' said rule-master, Tiegan. 'You lost that game fair and square.'

'OK, I admit it,' accepted Jayden, bending down to pick up the fallen pieces. 'I actually knew the second I touched it that I was doomed.'

Helping him gather up the scattered blocks with Ethan and Tiegan, Cleo asked Jayden if he could tell them about his story.

It had been over a month since Jayden had been surprised by Darryl with news of his one-on-one session with the author. Jayden had been so nervous to tell him about his idea. He thought that Leo Sparks would just be encouraging for the sake of it, like when your mum tells you you're the best poet in the world because you rhymed boom with zoom. But there was nothing fake about Leo Sparks. As Jayden had told him about his idea, he had rubbed his stubble thoughtfully and listened to every word.

'Well, Jayden,' he had said. 'I am a firm believer that the best stories are the ones based on what you know. And you have certainly put that into practice here.'

Jayden had repeated Leo's comments over and over again in his head since their meeting.

'But,' Leo had said, 'now, you need to use that amazing imagination of yours to make it even better. And I'm going to help you with that right now.'

Leo had spent a whole hour with Jayden bouncing ideas around. He had come away with a notepad full of inspiration, but even better than that, he had an entire plan for his story. And Leo had seemed one hundred percent genuine when he had told Jayden how great he thought it was going to be. Leo Sparks had told him that his story was going to be great! A real-life famous author had told him that his story was going to be great!! He couldn't believe it.

'OK' said Jayden to his friends. 'Well, it's a story about four children. They have to cope with some hard stuff at home, but then they meet each other, and everything starts to feel that little bit better.' He paused as he looked at the three pairs of eyes watching him intently. 'One of them is a bit bossy,' he continued, 'and thinks she's the leader of the group. One of them is really funny and talented at making people laugh. One of them cares so much about other people that she is the definition of kindness. She's also great with surprises. And one is a kind of angry boy who has all kinds of pent-up frustration until he meets the others, who accept him just as he is. They all find out they have superpowers like strength – but strength of mind rather than body. And the power of empathy – like they can really understand how someone else feels, almost like reading their mind.'

'Can they fly?' interrupted Ethan.

'No, they can't fly,' said Jayden. 'I thought that would be a bit of a cliché superpower. But they do have the power of resilience. No matter what obstacles they face, they just get straight back up and fight some more.'

'They sound awesome,' said Tiegan. 'Except for the bossy one. She sounds like a bit of a pain.'

Cleo raised her eyebrows at Jayden and giggled.

'What's so funny?' demanded Tiegan.

'Didn't you think the characters sounded familiar?' Ethan asked, also seeing through Jayden's character descriptions.

'Well, I guess you did win the talent show when you roasted the teachers last year,' admitted Tiegan. 'And Cleo is great with surprises. And Jayden was most definitely angry when we first found him in the yurt!'

Tiegan's mouth opened wide as she realised that this just left the bossy character. 'I am NOT bossy!' she exclaimed as the penny dropped.

'Well, you are a bit,' said Cleo, putting her arm round her friend. 'But every good squad needs a leader, right?'

'Right,' agreed Tiegan. 'And I am the oldest after all.'

'Exactly,' said Jayden, not wanting to offend his friend, who was indeed very bossy but also incredibly kind and caring with it. 'So, what do you think?' he asked. 'I just need to do one final edit on it and then I want you guys to help me decide on a title.'

'I think it sounds amazing!' said Cleo.

'Yep, it's gonna be brilliant!' agreed Ethan.

'One hundred percent,' concluded Tiegan. 'You will be the youngest author ever to sell millions of books and be able to afford a mansion.'

Jayden smiled bashfully at his friends. He

had never shown anyone his writing before as he was too worried that it wasn't as good as he had hoped. But he had just been given the seal of approval from three people whose opinion meant even more to him than a famous author. Three friends that he didn't even know he needed in his life until a few months ago. Three friends who made everything seem that little bit more normal.

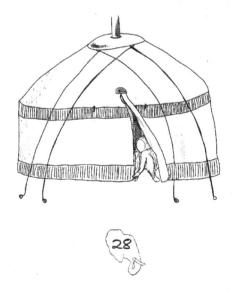

FUR THERAPY

'I really need to get home to my mum,' said Cleo, looking worried. 'She knows that school's finishing early today. She'll be expecting me.'

It was the last day of term, and Darryl had sent a message to the children's teachers telling them that The Elephant Squad were to meet him in the yurt before heading home for the summer.

'He probably just wants to make sure we're all going to keep in touch over the summer,' said Tiegan.

'Maybe suggest a new base for us to meet at whilst we can't use the yurt when the school's closed?' suggested Jayden.

'I'm sure he won't be long. Why don't you call your mum and let her know you'll be a little longer?' suggested Ethan.

Just as Cleo was punching the first few numbers into the safe to get the phone, Darryl poked his head into the yurt.

'Don't worry about calling your mum,' he reassured Cleo, knowing exactly what she was doing. 'She knows that you'll be a little later than you said.'

Cleo looked at Darryl, puzzled as to how her mum would know that.

'I spoke to her this morning,' he clarified.

Why would Darryl be calling my mum, she thought. But before she could ask, she heard a little whimper from outside. Darryl, who was still standing with just his head poking in, looked behind him.

'Come on, boy, let's go and say hello.'

As he walked into the yurt, the children all gasped as a little puppy on a lead hesitantly followed him in.

'Oh, my goodness,' said Cleo rushing over. 'He's adorable! Can I pick him up?'

Without waiting for an answer, she scooped the puppy up into her arms and it immediately began to lick her nose. The other children all rushed over to stroke him too. He was mostly white with patches of black, and his floppy ears and wagging tail looked too long for his little body.

'What kind of dog is he?' asked Cleo.

'I'm not entirely sure,' said Darryl. 'The rescue centre thinks he has a bit of Labrador in him and maybe some Collie.'

'He is just so cute,' continued Cleo, not caring that the puppy was slobbering all over her.

'What's his name?' asked Ethan.

'I thought Cleo could choose one,' said Darryl, winking at Tiegan, Ethan, and Jayden, who all smiled back knowingly.

They had all been privy to the reason why Darryl had asked them here, even if Cleo was in the dark.

'Really?' asked Cleo in wonder. She had thought long and hard about dog names since her mistake of calling her toy puppy Carol. She wouldn't make that mistake again.

'Does Mr Growler know that he's here?' Cleo suddenly asked, worried. Their head teacher had enforced a strict 'no dogs' rule when lots of parents had started bringing dogs to the playground to meet their children at pick-up time.

'Oh, yes, Mr Growler knows,' said Darryl smiling. 'And he knows that he is going to be seeing a lot more of him round here too.'

Cleo pulled her eyes away from the puppy long enough to look questioningly at Darryl.

'Why?' she asked.

'Because, Cleo, this little puppy here is going to be the school therapy dog!'

Cleo gasped in delight as she heard this.

Darryl had told them about a school that he visited where they had a therapy dog and she had always felt jealous. He had told them how when children are feeling sad or anxious, they are allowed to spend some time with the dog. Apparently stroking its fur has a calming effect that can soothe and reduce anxiety. Cleo felt her body relaxing as she held the puppy in her arms with his soft fur against her face. She couldn't quite believe that they were going to be lucky enough to have a therapy dog at their school!

'But where's he going to go when we're not here?' asked Cleo, frowning. She couldn't imagine Mr Growler having a pet dog. 'Surely someone has to look after him.'

'OK, Cleo, here's the thing,' said Darryl unable to keep the grin from his face. 'You care about everyone. You selflessly help your mum every day. You had the idea to bring the movie night to the yurt because Ethan missed out on going to the cinema.

You had the idea of creating a memory book for Tiegan. You are always putting others before yourself.'

Cleo felt her cheeks blushing as Darryl showered her with compliments. She felt awkward, not knowing quite how to take them and also having no idea where Darryl was heading with this.

'And I seem to remember you mentioning dogs like a billion times since I met you.'

Cleo giggled. It was true.

'We know you called your toy dog Carol,' said Jayden, laughing.

'And you told us dogs were your favourite animal,' said Tiegan.

'And you told us that if you were to take part in the school talent show, you'd want to do tricks with a dog,' said Ethan.

Cleo's cheeks turned an even deeper red as she realised that she had confided more in these friends in the last few months than she had in anyone, ever.

'And we know that you fantasise about

coming home to a dog as well as your mum when you rush home from school,' added Darryl gently.

'Well, I guess having a dog at school is almost as good as that,' said Cleo.

Her friends laughed as Cleo looked at them, still missing the point that they were trying to make.

'Cleo,' said Darryl. 'It's time for us to do something nice for you. You get to choose this puppy's name because, as well as being the school therapy dog, this puppy is yours!'

Cleo looked at Darryl in disbelief. 'What do you mean, he's mine?' she asked, not daring to let herself believe what her brain was slowly starting to register.

'I arranged it with your mum a few weeks ago, Cleo, and I let these guys in on the secret yesterday. This little puppy is *your* puppy. You get to feed him and stroke him and love him, and even let him sleep on the end of your bed if your mum will let you. Plus, you get to bring him into school every day to give other kids some much-needed fur therapy.'

Finally, it dawned on Cleo – the enormity of what Darryl and the original members of The Elephant Squad had surprised her with. As tears of happiness flowed down her cheeks and she muttered thank you over and over again, she knew exactly what she was going to call this new love of her life.

'OK, then, let me introduce you all to the newest member of The Elephant Squad - everyone, meet Ivory!

Other books by Kerry Gibb

Finalist IAN Book of the Year Awards 2018

Get signed copies of all Kerry Gibb's books from kerrygibb.com! Just scan the QR code.

Book for the mums! Kayla's Girls

If your mum enjoyed reading this with you, then tell her there's a book by Kerry Gibb just for her called Kayla's Girls! She can scan the QR code to find it!

Turn the page for a sneak preview of It's A Kid's Life...

Sneak preview of the first book in the It's A Kid's Life series!

It's A Kid's Life

Hi, I'm Ben Collins. I'm just a nine-year-old boy muddling my way through being a kid. Grown-ups always tell us that these are the best years of our lives, but as all us kids know, this is just a reflection of how forgetful parents can be as being a kid is hard!

Especially when you have three younger brothers to contend with like I do. I get the blame for EVERYTHING, just because I'm the oldest and 'should know better'. If they aren't trying to get me into trouble, then they are trying to wreck all my stuff. It drives me crazy!

I have recently come up with a solution to this problem though. I have this really cool intruder alarm on my door. I wanted a proper lock, but Mum told me that wasn't going to happen so this is the next best thing. If one of my brothers tries to enter my room uninvited, then a siren as loud as ten police cars fills the house. I get to run straight to my bedroom to catch the intruder red handed! The only problem is that I sometimes set the alarm before I go to bed and when Mum comes to check on me, she gets the fright of her life as the siren wails and has to spend the next hour getting my baby brother back to sleep. Oops!

Then there is school! Who on earth came up with the idea of sending all of us kids to school for five out of seven days a week? That is five days at school and two days at home. Who did the maths on that one? It is so not fair!

Anyway, that's enough of me moaning. You will get the wrong idea if I carry on moaning. I'm actually quite a happy sort of guy, despite all the hardship that comes along with being a kid. So, I'm going to give you a list of my favourite things to let you see what I'm really like.

1.   Computer games – I absolutely could not live without playing them. Maybe I could even invent my own one day!

2.   My dog – the best dog in the world, Obi!

3.   Pyjama Days – why get dressed when you aren't leaving the house? It makes getting ready for bed later a whole lot quicker!

4.   Chocolate – hey, what kid doesn't like chocolate? The bigger the bar, the better!

5.   Karate – Mum tells me that this is important for

discipline. I think it's great as you get to punch the Sensei's big fat belly to practice your skills.

6. Salmon – ha, you weren't expecting that one, were you? Just checking you were paying attention! Of course, I don't like salmon – yuck!

7. Play fighting with my brothers – ok so they are good for something!

8. Making money – I plan on being a millionaire by the time I am eighteen and if you carry on reading this book you will find out how!

So, there you have it. This is me and this is my story. Only things are about to get even harder for me as my mum and dad have made the crazy decision to move house which means that I have to start a new school! Needless to say, I am NOT impressed!

To continue reading, get your copy now from
kerrygibb.com and all good bookshops!

Discover the It's a Kid's Life series...

It's A Kid's Life

Ben Collins is your typical nine year old boy, muddling his way through life. As if being a kid isn't hard enough, his parents have just forced him to start a new school!

Read about his adventures here as he plans to make his millions by running a secret school tuck shop!

Bring into the equation a snowball fight, the most epic sickie ever, his trusty dog, Obi, and the distraction of the beautiful Lottie Jones, and you will soon see that things never quite go to plan!

It's A Kid's Life – Arch-Enemies

Just when Ben thinks that being a kid couldn't get any tougher, he finds that he has an arch-enemy! When she sabotages his school tuck shop, he faces the wrath or his headmaster, Mr Growler, who bans him from the school talent show.

How will he ever impress Lottie Jones if he can't perform his amazing, daring act? Will he find a way around his punishment? Will he ever think of a way to get back at his arch-enemy? With a little help from his best friend, Tommy, and his little brother, Pocket Rocket, maybe he will!

It's A Kid's Life – Double Digits

The summer holidays are here, and Ben Collins has finally turned ten! With his secret school tuck shop off limits for six weeks, Ben, and his best friend, Tommy, need to come up with other money making ideas.

Join them on a summer of excitement as they put their entrepreneurial skills to the test in their quest to become millionaires one day. Just don't tell Mum if they decide to make some quick money selling one of Ben's annoying younger brothers on the internet!

It's A Kid's Life - Christmas Countdown

Ben Collins has always loved the month of December. Chocolate advent calendars... dazzling tree lights...two whole weeks off school...and, in the words of his jealous little brother, two big presents on Christmas Day, thanks to having two dads!

His favourite month of the year gets even more exciting when he hears about the local newspaper competition to write the best article ever and win the prize money! Now all he needs to do is come up with a unique idea. Just when he thinks there is nothing worthy of originality, he sees something that is sure to win him first place... or is it?

It's A Kid's Life - Camp Chaos

Ben Collins is finally escaping his annoying little brothers for the week!

Join him and his friends on their much anticipated Year Six camp to the Isle of Wight. Be prepared for fearless 'truth or dare' escapades and exhilirating tests of courage that push the boundaries to the limit.

Throw into the mix a thunderstorm, an accident that could have ended in tragedy, and a brave display of true loyalty, and you will have a school camp that will go down in history!

KERRY GIBB
Illustrated by Brian Poole

MESSAGE FROM THE AUTHOR

Hi! I really hope you enjoyed reading this book. I love to hear from my readers, both children and their parents, so please do get in touch to let me know what you thought of it.

Did you know I have a VIP readers club on my website? You can join other children who get top secret insights and are the first to hear the latest news on all my books! Just ask your parents to email kerry@kerrygibb.com to join.

It would be fantastic if you could leave a review on Amazon. Children and parents are always looking for new books to read so it would be great if you let people know your thoughts. You can also leave your own review on my website at www.kerrygibb.com.

You can find me on Facebook and Instagram under 'Kerry Gibb Author' and my Twitter handle is AuthorKerryGibb.

ABOUT THE AUTHOR

Kerry Gibb is a mum to four boys. Their never-ending antics and awesome sense of humour gave her all the inspiration she needed to start writing children's books.

Kerry graduated from The University Of Sussex in 1999 with a degree in Social Psychology, where she took a particular interest in the development of children. She now regularly visits schools to promote reading and writing to children and inspire all the budding authors out there.

Kerry's favourite saying is 'Reach for the moon and even if you miss you will be among the stars.'

Acknowledgments

I always tell children that the best way to start a story is to base it on something that you know and then let the inspiration flow. The idea for this book grew from a conversation with a lady about young carers that she worked with. When I heard about their amazing courage, I knew that I just had to write this story. Thank you, Vicki Hannay, for igniting the spark that became The Elephant Squad.

Thank you to all my boys, Liam, Jamie, Danny, and Joe! Danny, in particular for being the first to read The Elephant Squad before it even had a name and give me the most valuable and honest feedback that you will only get from your own child! And also Joe, who at nine years old embraced the full process of my story creating, loving every word that I read to him as the story took shape and giving me the confidence to believe in it.

Thank you to my illustrator, Naomi Bunyan, for having the passion and enthusiasm to dive right into this project with me. She wowed me from her first picture she tentatively sent me of the butterfly on the book! And a huge thank you to her husband, Grant, whose graphic design expertise was invaluable!

Thank you to my editor, Bex Browne, for being one of life's lovely people and bringing her perfection to my words.

Thank you to Melina Alexandrou at The Honeypot Children's Charity for instantly feeling a connection to the story and seeing how great a charity partnership would be.

Thank you to you, the reader. Seeing children enjoy my books means the world to me. I hope you enjoyed reading it as much as I enjoyed writing it.

And leaving the most important to last, thank you to all the young carers out there. Never underestimate how amazing you truly are!